ELKAN

ELKAN

the adventure of a lifetime

JOHN & KATHY EYTCHISON

TATE PUBLISHING & Enterprises

TATE PUBLISHING
& Enterprises

Tate Publishing is committed to excellence in the publishing industry. Our staff of highly trained professionals, including editors, graphic designers, and marketing personnel, work together to produce the very finest books available. The company reflects the philosophy established by the founders, based on Psalms 68:11,

"THE LORD GAVE THE WORD AND GREAT WAS THE COMPANY OF
THOSE WHO PUBLISHED IT."

If you would like further information, please contact us:

1.888.361.9473 | www.tatepublishing.com

TATE PUBLISHING *& Enterprises*, LLC | 127 E. Trade Center Terrace
Mustang, Oklahoma 73064 USA

Published in the United States of America

ISBN: 978-1-6024732-3-2

07.04.23

This book is dedicated to Evan and James, and anyone else who is willing to take "The Adventure of a Lifetime."

ACKNOWLEDGMENTS

We would like to give special thanks to everyone who helped and encouraged us along our journey of writing this book. You know who you are.

To Dan, this is all your fault for giving us that first nudge. Look what you started!

So, a super special thanks to Steven to thank you for revealing some refinements we had to make. You know what we mean.

To the "Omi & Pa Hotel," for the many vacancies and taxi services provided for peace and quiet.

A very special thanks to Ken Ham for his legacy and example. A true inspiration.

Finally, and most importantly, to the One who made this all possible. Your words and inspiration carried us through.

THANK YOU!

TABLE OF CONTENTS

FOREWORD

Prior to missionaries leaving for the field to share the Gospel, they endure a lot of training. As a minimum, they learn the language and culture in order to be effective. Unfortunately in America today, Christians need to learn a new language and culture to have our message understood.

For the most part, young people today love adventure and fantasy yet are Biblically illiterate. John and Kathy have written an adventure that will challenge and entertain young people.

Elkan's adventure will help train this next generation to the fact that God's Word is true. I pray that many young people in our world today will experience the same joy that Elkan finds on his journey through the Word of God! Good job, John and Kathy, for using a language our culture understands to communicate this important message.

Carl D. Kerby
Founding Director/International Speaker
Answers in Genesis
Author of: *Remote Control: The Power of Hollywood on Today's Culture*

CHAPTER I

UNEXPECTED JOURNEY

On the outskirts of Arborstead, down a rugged dirt road, stands an ancient church. Although still used by the townspeople, its glory days of 200 years ago are long gone. The white buttermilk paint is cracked and chipping. Two of the four shutters are hanging by one hinge and a third is lying on the ground below the window it used to shield. The stained glass images of Adam and Eve, Noah, the nativity, and crucifixion are dirty and dingy. The front steps sit crooked and uneven. It's not that unusual to see the occasional church mouse running in or out of the holes in the stone foundation. To the left of the church is a cemetery full of old, half-sunken tombstones faintly bearing the names of some of the town's founding fathers. A short, black cast iron fence surrounds the cemetery. To the right of the church is a knee-high, weather beaten and moss-covered rock wall made of the same kinds of stones as the church foundation. Beside the rock wall stands a row of tall, old oak trees that have been there since before the time the church was built.

Rain is pouring down. This is the worst storm Arborstead

JOHN *and* KATHY EYTCHISON

has seen in years. Inside the church, Elkan Abrams is helping Mrs. Brown, his Sunday school teacher, clean the classroom. As he is replacing the chairs around the tables, water starts to drip from the ceiling.

"Elkan," asks Mrs. Brown, "would you run to the basement and grab a bucket for that leak, please?"

"Sure Mrs. Brown," Elkan replies.

Elkan runs down the hall toward the basement door. He places his hand on the antique brass doorknob and turns it. The door creaks and pops as it opens. He cautiously makes his way down the damp stone steps into the dark basement. As he approaches the bottom of the steps, he reaches his hand up, moves his arm around in circles until he feels a string dangling from the ceiling. He grabs it and pulls. A single, not very bright light bulb flickers on. The dimly lit basement reveals tiny streams of water trickling in through the foundation, finally resting in a couple puddles on the hard dirt floor.

Elkan looks around for the bucket. He sees a mop and other cleaning supplies on a shelf against the back wall. He heads to the back of the basement in hopes that the bucket is there too. As he walks past piles of boxes on another set of shelves, he catches a glimpse of a slight gold shimmer. Intrigued, Elkan investigates the glimmering object.

Picking up one box and moving it, then another, Elkan finds a large old book lying on its side with the spine facing the wall. The gold shimmer is from the edges of the pages of the book that are facing out. He pulls the book off the shelf and brushes the dust and cobwebs off the cover.

"This has got to be the oldest book I have ever seen," he says softly to himself. "I wonder what it's about! Maybe there's a treasure map in it! Or maybe a secret message!"

The book is hard leather bound and plain. No title on the cover. No title on the spine. Elkan finds a pile of boxes to set the book on because of its size and weight. As he opens the cover of the book, for a split instant the basement gets very bright and then a loud CRACK and POP, then sudden darkness. Another round of lightning illuminates the basement through the small glass windows toward the ceiling just long enough for Elkan to read the words, "In the beginning" in old English script; then darkness again.

Not able to see a thing, Elkan feels a light mist of water on his face. It feels like he's dizzy or that the floor is rocking slightly to and fro. He hears the creaking of wood and what sounds like the gentle rolling of waves.

Ka-Klunk. Ka-Klunk. Ka-Klunk.

Elkan hears footsteps behind him. "Mrs. Brown? Is that you?" he asks timidly.

"No, Elkan," a deep gentle, yet commanding, voice replies. "My name is Captain Kamali." A dim flickering light appears behind Elkan.

As Elkan turns to see who or what is behind him, he is met with a lantern. Its jumping flame softly glows on the face of a tall, well-built man with a rigid jaw. He has a pleasant and kind appearance. His hair is dark and wavy with sideburns that come half way down his cheek. He is well groomed and has a slight cleft in his chin.

Elkan turns quickly to run from the stranger not knowing what's in front of him when he feels a strong tug on his shirt and can't run at all. The man grabs his shirt and holds him back.

"Wha ... Wh ... Wh ... Who are you?" tremors Elkan.

"My name is Kamali. I need your help Elkan."

"How ... do you ... know ... my ... name? Why is the floor ... moving? I think I feel sick!"

A loud, deep, imposing voice fills the air and vibrates in Elkan's chest. "*Let there be light!*"

In an instant the whole of the sky lights up and everything around Elkan is visible.

"Whoa! What just happened, man?" exclaims Elkan!

"You may address me as Captain—Captain Kamali. You just came into the first day, that's what happened."

Elkan looks around and only sees water from horizon to horizon. He's on a ship in the middle of the ocean.

"How did I end up on a ship? What do you mean the first day? Where's land? Where's my church? Where's Mrs. Brown? Take me back!"

"Elkan, you must listen to me. There is no going back. You are starting a new life. Your old life is gone. You'll understand in time. You must trust me!"

"Trust you? How can I trust you when I don't even know who you are? You kidnap me, bring me out to the middle of the ocean, and expect me to trust you?"

"Look around you Elkan! Look and tell me what you see. Don't look at what you think you see, but look at the truth of things as God reveals it to you. Let me help you. Yes, you're on a ship. The name of this ship is *The Spirit of God.* This ship is moving upon the face of the waters. Tell me what you truly see, Elkan!"

Elkan pauses, looks around, and starts describing what he sees. "I see you! You are dressed in some old-fashioned uniform with a really old hat and hair style."

"That's a start, Elkan, but tell me the minute details of what you really see. Don't just tell me what you see on the surface."

"Man, you sound like my teachers! I see you wearing a blue coat with fat lapels. Your collar is gold trimmed and standing up to your jaw. Your lapels are also gold trimmed with a gazillion gold buttons. You have those stringy lace shoulder pads on your shoulders. Your cuffs are also gold trimmed with gold buttons. You're wearing white pants, black shoes, a black belt and another white coat underneath your blue one. You also have a sword. There! Is that better?"

"Yes, Elkan. Excellent start. Now, again, tell me what you see all around you."

"What's this got to do with anything? I'm not supposed to be here! I'd really like to know how I got here! And I still don't understand what's going on!"

Kamali places his hands on Elkan's shoulders in a fatherly manner and gently explains; "Son, do not be afraid! I am here to protect you and guide you. Trust what I tell you and do as I say and you will remain safe and gain wisdom. You are here for a reason. I understand your confusion and fear. Walk with me Elkan."

As they start walking toward the front of the ship Elkan lifts his head and looks up. All he sees are huge sails.

"Wow!" Elkan gasps against the rustling and snapping of the sails. "How big are those things?"

"Large enough to carry us to where the east and the west meet!"

The two stop and look out over the deck as far as the eye can see. Elkan hears the creaking wood and gentle rolling of the waves, just as he heard earlier in the dark.

"Now, I'd like to show you something Elkan."

"What is it?"

"Follow me."

They head below the deck to the captain's quarters and Kamali shows Elkan a highly decorated chest with seven locks.

"I knew it! I knew you had some kind of treasure chest on board!" exclaims Elkan.

"This is why you are here, Elkan. This chest contains some very precious cargo and I need your help to safely get it where it's going. Notice that there are seven locks. Each one requires a different key. We must find those keys so that we can open the chest and deliver the cargo to its owner."

Elkan studies the chest very closely. It stands about two feet high, two feet deep, and approximately four feet long. It has a flat top. There is gold gilt and decoration all around it, from top to bottom. There are gold heads on the lid; an ox, lion, eagle, and a man's all connected at the top of the head but looking in four different directions. The same image is on both ends of the lid. There are two large gold rings on each end of the chest. And then there are the seven locks. Each one is a different shape and size. They each also have their own individual and unique symbol on the face of the lock.

The first lock is quartz with a capital "A" on it.

The second lock is heavily rusted and corroded. There is no symbol on it, just a plain simple lock totally consumed in rust.

The third lock is made of bronze. The symbol is a series of seven half circles, one inside the other.

The fourth lock is a square stone block with a different pyramid etched into each side.

The fifth lock is wooden and has the image of a six-pointed star carved into it.

The sixth lock is stone and in the shape of a dome. A second, donut-shaped stone is in the middle and is almost the size of the lock itself. It appears that the donut hole is the keyhole.

And finally, the last lock is gold with beautiful colorful stones embedded in it. It is cube shaped and each side has three lines of multiple symbols–like hieroglyphics. The top and bottom are encrusted in the same colorful stones and the bottom contains the keyhole.

"So where do we find the keys?" Elkan asks inquisitively.

"That, my dear boy, is what we have to discover! We will be sailing seven seas, and we will find them during our voyage through each sea. I can also tell you this; we will only find them when the time is right and that will be determined by you. Come over to my table and let me show you something else."

Elkan walks over to the captain's table while Kamali removes an old painting of a beautiful golden and jeweled city on a hill from the wall. Behind the painting is a door with a lock on it. Kamali opens a small leather bag attached to his side and pulls out a key, inserts it into the lock and turns it. The lock falls open and he removes it from the door. Kamali opens the door, reaches in and pulls out a long roll of parchment paper. Kamali carries it over to the captain's table where Elkan is standing, sets it on one side and unrolls it across the table. The size of the map takes up almost the entire top of the table.

Elkan's eyes widen with excitement as he watches. As the map unrolls he sees what is ahead of him - the Sea of Creation, the Sea of Corruption, and the Sea of Catastrophe. Each one with its place on the map with a small illustration of things Elkan doesn't understand. Further unrolling of the map reveals the Sea of Confusion, the Sea of Christ and the Sea of The Cross. Elkan is intrigued that the Sea of The Cross is actually in the shape of a cross and is colored a pale red. Finally, as the last portion of the map is unrolled, he sees the Sea of Consummation. The bottom left corner of the map has the Compass Rose with images of dolphins above it. The middle of the map shows an image of a ship with its crew battling a large sea monster, and the narrow inlet to the Sea of Consummation shows a picture of what looks like a Plesiosaur. Elkan and Kamali spend the rest of the day going over the map with Kamali explaining what certain things are, but also leaving some things vague saying something about being a babe on milk and not ready for meat yet.

Elkan loses track of time while pouring over the map when Kamali breaks in and says, "It is evening and time to turn in and get some rest."

Kamali leads Elkan to his sleeping quarters. They are certainly not what he is used to at home. There is no real bed with a mattress, only a hammock hanging from the walls and an old feather pillow. As Kamali leaves the room, he blows out the lantern by the door and turns back toward Elkan. The vague silhouette against the dimly lit outer room says, "Get a good night's rest Elkan. We have a long journey ahead of us."

With that, the door to the room clamors shut. The room is pitch black. The rocking and creaking of the ship quickly soothes Elkan to sleep.

The next morning Elkan awakens to the sound of rushing water. He heads up to the deck to find out what it is. As he walks out onto the deck he sees walls of water all around the boat.

"Kamali!" Elkan yells, "Kamali, where are you?"

"I'm right here Elkan." Kamali replies from behind. "Interesting isn't it? Have you ever seen such a thing?"

"No! What's happening? Are we going through a waterfall?"

"Look up. Do you see water coming down from above us? Are we getting wet?

"No. How is that happening?"

"Watch the wall of water very closely. What do you see?"

"It looks like a solid wall of water. You can't see five feet out from the ship. It's like the ocean is surrounding us except from above."

"Yes ... "

"Wait! The water is actually moving up—up to the sky! It's like a reverse rain, like super-high-power evaporation."

"Remember last night when I told you that we would journey seven seas?

"Yes."

"Well, this is your second day on the Sea of Creation. During our voyage you will witness strange but wonderful things as they are revealed to you, true things."

"Like what?"

"I can't tell you everything Elkan. Just be observant and learn and remember what you see, hear, and experience. Let's take a tour of the ship. We'll start at the beginning - the front of the ship."

Kamali and Elkan walk to the front of the ship.

"We will use the deck of the ship as a reference point," Kamali starts. "The deck is the top level of the ship, as you probably know. When you're on the deck you're said to be 'above deck.' The front of the ship is the bow, or fore, and the back of the ship is the stern, or aft. Each of the long poles, or spars, that hold the sails is called a mast. You have the main part of the mast secured to the deck, an additional spar on top called the topmast, and a third spar that can be placed on top of that called the topgallant. The one at the front of the ship pointing forward is called the bowsprit. Below it on the front of the ship is a figure of an angel. You can't see her very well, but you will see her beauty when we dock and you look on from land. She is called the figurehead. The foremost mast is called the foremast."

Elkan and Kamali walk toward midship and on toward the back of the ship as Kamali explains along the way, "The mast in the middle of the ship is called the mainmast. The mast behind the mainmast is called the mizzenmast. Finally, the last upright mast at the stern of the ship is called the bonaventure mizzenmast."

As they reach the rear of the ship, Kamali points to a pole sticking out of the back similar to the one up front, "The mast sticking out from the stern of the ship is called the outrigger."

Kamali turns back toward the rest of the ship and continues, "Each sail has its own name according to which mast it is on. Finally, all of the ropes that you see going from spar to spar and deck to spar are called the rigging. The rigging is used to support the masts and move the sails. You will also notice some rope ladders that are used to get up the masts. Those are called 'Jacob's Ladders.' You will also notice the crow's nest at the top of the main mast."

Awestruck and curious Elkan asks, "So, are all of the sails up now?"

"Not all of them, but many of them are," Kamali replies. "Are you ready to head below?"

"Sure!"

They stroll back to midship and open the hatch to head below deck. Kamali explains that there are four levels below deck and shows Elkan the galley, or kitchen; the cabins; the sick bay; the bunks, and finally they end up at the captain's quarters, all along explaining what each part of the ship is and how it works.

Elkan notices how nice the captain's quarters are compared to the other cabins and bunks. The back wall is glass and overlooks the ocean where the ship has been. You can see the wake in the water from the ship. On the far side of the room is a bed that is a large feather mattress on a bed frame. The chest with the seven locks is at the foot of the bed while a plain wooden trunk is next to the wardrobe opposite the bed. There are bookshelves, the captain's own dining table, and lots of room to spread out. It's even larger than Elkan's room back home, which gets him wondering about home.

"How long will this voyage be, Captain?" asks Elkan.

"Oh, it will be some time. We will spend a week on the Sea of Creation alone. We are only just over 24 hours into the journey. Then we have the other six seas to sail. Those seas I can't tell you how long they will take. It will depend upon how quickly we can find the keys–and that will also depend upon you.

"Why don't I let you explore the ship a little Elkan? I'll find you after a while."

So Elkan sets out to explore the ship. After losing track of time, he hears Kamali call for him. They meet and go to the galley to make a sandwich for dinner.

"Well, Elkan, it is evening and you've had a long day exploring the ship. You've learned a lot, but now it is time to turn in. Do you remember the way back to your bunk?"

"Yes, I'm pretty sure I do."

"Then I will see you in the morning, Elkan."

And Kamali escorts Elkan to the door.

Elkan heads back to his bunk, climbs into his hammock, blows out his candle and closes his eyes. Again, the gentle creaking and rocking of the ship quickly puts him to sleep.

CRASH!

Elkan jumps awake, hits his head, and falls out of his hammock. He rolls across the floor, hits the wall, and starts rolling back. He stumbles to his feet only to lose his balance and fall again, catching himself on his hammock.

The ship is being tossed back and forth like a cowboy on a bucking bronco and Elkan can barely keep his balance as he heads to the stairs to go above deck. He decides to check around the ship for Kamali first, thinking that he probably isn't above deck with the ship being tossed like it is. He checks everyplace he knows of, calling for Kamali with no answer. Finally, he decides Kamali must be above deck so he heads back to the hatch.

As Elkan opens the hatch, water comes rushing in and knocks him to the floor. Regaining his composure, Elkan tries opening the hatch again. This time he succeeds, but with a face full of water and drenched clothes. Once he is above deck, he sees Kamali standing at the bow of the ship with the waves just missing him. Elkan makes his way, stumbling and slipping, to Kamali.

"Look Elkan! Isn't it just gorgeous?" Kamali exclaims as he points off in the distance.

"All I see are huge waves that are crashing down on us!" Elkan says in bewilderment. "Is there a storm coming? I don't see anything!"

"Here, take my telescope and see for yourself!"

As Elkan looks through the shiny brass telescope he sees land far off in the distance.

"Keep watching, Elkan! You'll see something amazing!"

Elkan continues looking through the scope when the ship takes a huge hit from a gigantic wave. Knocking him off balance, he falls into the arms of Kamali. As they regain their composure, they notice, a couple hundred meters off the bow of the ship, land rising out of the water.

"Avast," Kamali yells! "Avast!"

The ship starts slowing down. The land gets higher and closer.

"It's a volcano! We're gonna hit it," Elkan screams!

"Alas! Land!" Kamali sighs heavily. "Do not worry Elkan. It's not a volcano and the ship will stop before we run aground."

"What about *it* hitting us?"

"It won't! See, it has stopped and the waters are calming.

Look around! We are in a cove. Land surrounds us except for the entrance to the cove behind us."

All that Elkan can see is a beach that leads to more beaches. He sees nothing but beach–pebbles and dirt. There are no palm trees or patches of beach grass; there is nothing but earth. It is barren land for as far as his eyes can see.

"We will anchor momentarily," explains Kamali. "When we do, we will get in the dinghy and go ashore.

"By the way Elkan, I want you to have this," and he hands Elkan a small leather bag with a drawstring. "I want you to use this ditty bag to keep the keys in as we find them."

"Ditty bag?" Elkan snickers. "Okay!"

Elkan hears a splash and the clanking of a chain. The ship comes to a halt. The anchor is set. He and Kamali climb into the dinghy and lower it down to the water. As they head toward land Elkan looks back at the ship. For the first time he can see the ship from the outside looking on.

"Wow! How awesome!" Elkan marvels at the ship. "That thing is huge! It towers over us like a skyscraper!"

Passionately Kamali replies, "Yes, *The Spirit of God* is quite majestic and very glorious. It is a fortress in which I place my trust!"

As the dinghy rounds the bow of the ship, Elkan finally sees the figurehead of the ship, the angel.

In absolute astonishment Elkan gasps, "It's the most beautiful thing I've ever seen - The flowing hair and white robe, the golden wings and the gentleness and passion of the face, the bright and beautiful light from the sky behind it. Do you think that is what heaven looks like? But why is the angel holding a sword?"

Kamali utters, "An Angel before us to keep us in the way and to bring us into the place that He has prepared."

"What are you talking about?" Elkan asks confused.

Just then the dinghy comes upon the shore. They hop out and pull it up onto the pebble beach. Then they tie it to a larger rock about two feet high. The pebbles are smooth and marble-like. They glisten in the bright light from the dampness of the water. One stone, about the size of a quarter catches Elkan's eye. He picks it up. It is a beige color with a blood red swirl in it. *This is the perfect shape and size for a sling shot*, Elkan thinks to himself as he stuffs it in his ditty bag.

"Come along Elkan. Our days are but a breath and we have a lot to accomplish!"

So Elkan and Kamali head inland. As the stone beach becomes solid land, Elkan feels the softness of the ground beneath his feet. Footprints are starting to become impressed into what is now dirt. Three steps later Elkan notices a little green around his feet. Plants are sprouting. But there is nothing but earth ahead of them. No vegetation whatsoever. Elkan and Kamali take another step. Suddenly more plants start sprouting. With each step they take, more and more plants start to come forth from the earth. Perplexed, Elkan looks back and notices a path through a lush tropical field that leads back to the beach. The plants behind them are now knee high and still nothing but dirt in front of them.

"What's happening, Kamali?"

"You're experiencing day three Elkan. Observe. Use your senses. Use your mind. Again, I tell you, look at the truth of what you see, not just the surface of what you see or think you see. Learn and experience everything around you, Elkan. Everything you are experiencing is truth. Know it and remember it, always! Keep it in your heart!"

As they are walking, Elkan enjoys looking at the plants and flowers of all kinds and watching them appear beneath his feet. Plants and flowers he has never seen before. Some of them are strange and wonderful. Many of them smell fragrant and sweet. The aroma that fills the air is extremely pleasant to the senses. Some of the plants even have leaves that are fuzzy. They are very soft to the touch. There are plants with leaves and flowers of every color, shape, and size imaginable. Elkan can't believe his eyes.

Elkan quickly stops and thinks to himself. "Kamali told me to trust everything I'm experiencing. That means that I have to believe everything I see. But how can this be? I don't know what to believe right now. I can't even believe that all of this is happening. But I'm experiencing it, so it must be true."

All of a sudden it's dark—pitch black. Elkan trips and stumbles into Kamali. Within a few seconds Kamali has the lantern lit. The soft glow of the dimly lit flame flickers off the plants around them. They can only see within a few feet around them, but it's enough to see their path.

Before Elkan has a chance to say a word, Kamali commands, "It's night. Let's get back to the beach and set up camp."

As briskly as the lantern light will allow them, they walk back along their path to the beach. Elkan notices in the dimly lit shadows cast from the lantern that the plants have grown amazingly fast throughout the day. Some of them are as tall as he is and even taller. Kamali and Elkan get back to the pebble beach and set up camp. Along the way, Elkan is trying to figure out what happened to the daylight but all Kamali keeps telling him is that it is now nighttime.

Once back at camp, Kamali grabs two sacks from the dinghy, carries them up past the rock beach, and opens one. He pulls out three wood poles and a large canvas. One of the poles is longer than the other two. With the lantern on the ground, Kamali takes the three poles and places one end of each in the ground and brings the other ends together at the top making a pyramid. He ties the poles together with a rope. Then Kamali unrolls the canvas over the top of the longest pole and stakes it to the ground. "Here is your tent. It will keep the heavy dew off of you." Then Kamali sets up his tent.

Elkan lies down to rest for the night with his head at the opening of the tent and stares into the night sky to look at the stars. "Kamali," Elkan asks, "why aren't there any stars in the sky? I don't even see the moon. Where are they?"

"You will see them tomorrow." Kamali answers.

And with that, Kamali is asleep. Elkan is quite exhausted too, but he doesn't fall asleep right away. He lies there thinking about the past few days and everything that has happened. He thinks about home, about his dog Achaia, and his parents and friends–even his annoying little sister who doesn't seem quite as annoying now. He wonders about Kamali and why he is so vague about everything.

I have no real reason to trust him, Elkan thinks, *but I have no real reason not to either. He said he would protect me. He must know more than I do. I wonder what tomorrow is going to be like. How long will this journey last? I can't wait to tell everyone back home about this! But wait, Kamali said that this is my new life, and that I have left my old life behind.*

Realizing the situation, Elkan begins to weep quietly as to not awaken Kamali. He decides to say a little prayer to God and ask Him for understanding. Before a tear can hit the ground and before he can finish his prayer, exhaustion overtakes him and he falls asleep.

The waves softly roll upon the shore. Elkan slowly opens his eyes. There is a dim light in the sky. He looks out at the ship. Watching the waves gently chase each other across the sea, Elkan catches a glimpse of sunlight rising over the edge of the sea. As he walks toward the water, the sky turns yellow and red and orange and peach and purple and dark blue. It looks like a swirl of multicolored cotton candy. Then, a bright orange ball slowly rises over the horizon. This is the most exquisite and marvelous sunrise Elkan has ever seen or could even imagine. The orange ball reflects off the water as twinkles dance across the waves. The sea is golden.

"Most beautiful thing you've ever seen isn't it?" a gentle voice says from behind Elkan. "I know you don't understand a lot of things Elkan, but you will later. I know these things because I have been around for a long time and my Father taught me well. Your Father will teach you well too, so long as you listen and are obedient."

Elkan turns to see Kamali and behind him a forest of plants. There are even trees this time. Trees that have flowers and trees that have fruit. Elkan notices that the colors of the plants are of the most vivid colors anyone could imagine. There is a fog like mist on the ground about ankle high but getting higher and thicker as he looks further into the forest. Then he spots an apple tree. Quickly he jumps up and runs over to grab an apple. Each one is the perfect shape and a bright red. They look like something from a painting. He plucks one from the branch and bites into it. The juice squirts into his mouth and drips down his hand. It's tender and succulent.

"This apple is perfect! It's juicy and sweet and you don't break your teeth biting into it."

Kamali laughs.

"It is perfect isn't it? Don't get used to it though. Enjoy it while you can. Not to mention, are you sure it's an apple?"

"Of course I'm sure, it looks and tastes like one. It's just more tender and juicy."

"Look around, Elkan! All of this is perfect! Every fruit and vegetable you see, whether you recognize it or not, is edible - nothing poisonous or dangerous. It is all good!"

Elkan takes a long, thorough look around. He starts seeing things for the first time. He notices that the world around him is completely different from what he's used to. There are plants with vibrant colored leaves–red and purple and blue and yellow. It's almost as if the leaves of some of the plants are the flowers themselves. Most of the plants have green leaves, but they're not just green; they are true green. They are the most perfect green Elkan has ever seen. And it's not just seeing the color green, but knowing deep down inside that this is what green is supposed to be. The same is true for every color of plant or flower he sees.

Knowing that all of the fruit is safe, Elkan has a brilliant idea. He runs over to a tree that looks like a palm tree. He climbs it, grabs what looks to him like a coconut, and drops down out of the tree. Then he runs here and there and several different places collecting fruit. When he gets to the raspberries and blackberries he is very cautious not to get pricked by thorns. As he's plucking the berries he realizes something.

"Hey Captain! Come over here!"

"Yes, Elkan! What is it?"

"These berries are raspberries and blackberries right?"

"They do appear to be, why?"

"There's no thorns on the branches. Why not?"

"Ahh … you've noticed! You're starting to learn how to observe the truth around you as it is revealed. You will find that there are no thorns here! Remember, everything is perfect–Everything!"

"How can that be? There is no such thing as perfect!"

"That is where you are wrong, my son. Everything here is perfect and good, but the rest of our journey will not be this way. You are being blessed with the best in the beginning. Remember, you watched the miracle of all of this come into being, and you will see many more miracles over the next few days. Do you truly believe that Creation cannot be perfect, according to God's standards?"

"Well, yeah, but ... I'm just confused and don't completely understand what's going on."

"That's fine, Elkan. You are learning. You will understand what all of this is about in time."

Elkan picks the rest of his berries and then runs over to the campsite, drops all of the fruit in a pile and grabs the coconut.

"Hey, Cap'! Can you use your sword to hack open this coconut for me?"

"There is no need for that, Elkan. Pick it up and gently press and feel around the shell. Do you feel that?"

Elkan gently presses his fingers around the outside of the coconut. At one point he feels a dimple. Then he realizes the dimple is actually a groove going around the coconut.

"You've got to be kidding! Don't tell me I can open this coconut with my bare hands!" Elkan shouts in disbelief.

"It is true my boy. Try it."

Elkan presses his fingers harder along the groove and starts to pull each side apart. Struggling a little he feels a slight give and then a small hole opens from the top. Then he tilts the coconut on its side so that the groove is like a belt around it and he starts to pull some more. Slowly the top half of the shell comes off, leaving the bottom shell full of coconut milk.

Elkan then presses the shell into the ground a little to hold it upright so the milk won't spill. He takes the empty half and puts a mixture of the other fruits in it. Next he presses his fist down on the fruit to squish the juice out. When he's finally satisfied that he has squeezed enough juice out, he pours it into the other half of the coconut with the milk in it. Then he uses his stained fingers to stir the mixture.

Meanwhile, Kamali is standing a short distance behind Elkan watching him. He has a big smile on his face like a proud father.

"Hey, Cap'! You gotta try this!"

"What is it?"

"Well, it's kinda like a fruit smoothie just not frozen. It's really good!"

Kamali gives the concoction a try and nods his head with approval to the taste.

Elkan runs out to the beach to wash his hands in the ocean. The juice stains wash clean and disappear in the water almost immediately, like vanishing ink.

Elkan turns to Kamali in amazement. Kamali just smiles an all-knowing smile.

Kamali walks over to the campsite, picks up a leather bag with a cork in the opening and strolls over to the edge of the water. He bends down and submerges the bag into the ocean. As the air rushes from the bag, bubbles spew forth and the bag fills rapidly with water.

"What are you doing," Elkan asks bewildered?

"Gathering water for the day," Kamali gently replies.

"Gathering water for what?"

"To drink."

"To drink? You can't drink ocean water!"

"Why not, Elkan?"

"Because it's salty! It tastes nasty, and it'll dehydrate you!"

"Elkan! Stop and listen to what you are saying. Is it true? Do you know that for sure? Have you tasted the water yet? Think about what you are saying and think about where you are. Are there thorns on the berry bushes? Are all of the fruits and herbs safe to eat? Is this not the Lord's Perfect Creation? Forget what you think you know. You have left that life behind; remember? You're starting a new life. Think with a new mind. Understand things with your heart as well as your mind. Learn the truth of what you are experiencing. This is truth! Now, dip your hands into the water and bring them to your lips to drink."

Kamali then lifts the bulging bag to his lips and drinks, setting an example for Elkan to follow.

Seeing this, Elkan reluctantly dips his hands into the sea. Thinking to himself, *This is against my better judgment, but I have to trust him. He hasn't lied to me yet.* He cups his hands and brings the water up to his lips, touches his lips to the water, and sips.

"This is amazing! This is the best water I have ever tasted! It's so ... pure and ... clean! It's even better than bottled water!"

"Pure water, Elkan. You will never taste water that is more pure than this right here! Before we leave, we will have to fill our barrels stocking up on it, for it won't stay pure forever."

As the day passes, Elkan and Kamali explore the shoreline. It's beautiful and peaceful. The sun shines down, yet the temperature is perfect. It's not too hot, nor is it too cool. And there's not even a cloud in the sky. They also spend part of the day walking the path they created the day before, checking out the hundreds and thousands of different plants. Before they know it, the sun starts to set. The sky turns a golden orange and the sea looks like a sheet of gold and crystal. The temperature drops a little, but only to the level of the perfect spring evening—the perfect temperature to sleep.

After the sun sets, Elkan notices the biggest, brightest moon he could ever imagine. It looks like he could almost reach up and grab it. The moon is smooth, the perfect round white ball–like the perfect flawless pearl. Elkan doesn't even notice any of the shading he is used to seeing from the cratered surface. And the brightness, it's so bright that he can see everything around him. But the brilliance of the moon is nothing compared to that of the stars. The stars cover the sky. They are close together, like holes in a pitch-black screen. And they shine like water droplets filling each hole of that screen when the light catches them at just the right angle. They shine like flawless jewels - diamonds and rubies and sapphires and topaz.

Elkan and Kamali make camp and lie down for the night. Elkan lies on his back staring up at the exquisite night sky. He tries counting stars, but there are just too many. Instead, he lies there watching them twinkle, each as if they are winking just at him. As he falls asleep, he remembers a verse in his Bible, in Genesis. It says God made the sun and the moon, but then it says He made the stars also, as if they were an afterthought. How could such beauty and wondrous things be just an afterthought - especially if He has named each one?

The next morning Elkan wakes to the glow of the sunrise on his face again. But this time, the morning is also greeted with singing birds. He lies there for a few moments listening to the avian orchestra. Suddenly he hears a loud screech off in the distance.

Elkan quickly sits up and listens again. He hears nothing but birds singing. He lies back down and hears the screech again. Again, Elkan quickly gets up. This time he jumps to his feet and yells to Kamali, "Did you hear that, Captain?" There is no response from Kamali so Elkan looks over to where the captain sleeps, but he's not there. His heart racing, Elkan starts looking around. His mind is put to rest when he sees Kamali down by the edge of the sea. Elkan runs toward Kamali. Then he hears the screech again, this time it's much louder. Suddenly, from over the forest, a large reptile-like bird flies over their heads and out toward the ocean.

"What is that thing?" Elkan yells in fear. "It looks like a pteranodon!"

"It's simply a dragon my boy," Kamali replies. "A flying serpent."

"You mean the fire-breathing-village-attacking-people-eating kind of a dragon?"

"No! That particular one doesn't breathe fire. But later we may come across some that do."

"Okay, that's enough! I've had enough of all this strange stuff. I want to head back home! Let's get our stuff packed up, go back to the ship, and you can take me back home!"

"I'm sorry Elkan, that's not possible."

"What do you mean it's not possible?"

"Just what I said. You can't head back now."

"You've been telling me to look around at all this impossible stuff and to believe it as truth. You can't tell me that, with everything we have seen, taking me home is *impossible*!"

"With man it is impossible, but with God all things are possible. Everything you have seen and heard and experienced is possible because God has made it so. And for the same reason I can't take you back home, I am not God. He has you here for His purpose. If you truly decide to go back home, you will not have finished your journey and the precious cargo I have on the ship will never make it to its destination. Remember, Elkan, I need you to help me. Your decision will affect many people, directly and indirectly. Now, do you really want to give up and leave? Do you want to miss out on what is yet to come? Search your heart and then let me know. God will find another one who is willing to go for Him."

Elkan stomps off and heads back to camp. He hears another screech, then another and another. He lifts his head to the sky and sees several of the flying serpents as well as many other different types of birds and flying creatures. Some of them are small and some of them are large. Some of them are very colorful and some of them are plain in design.

Why aren't the flying serpents eating the smaller birds, Elkan wonders to himself.

Elkan sits on the pebble beach and looks down at the stones, studying them in detail. He sees a marbled gray oblong stone with an "X" on it so he picks it up. Studying the stone prompts him to think of the Ten Commandments. Then Elkan remembers Moses, the one who delivered the commandments to the Israelites. At first Moses didn't want to do what God had asked him to do, but ultimately he obeyed. That obedience led to many great things because God blessed his obedience. "If God has brought me on this journey, then who am I to question and disobey. If He is going to use me like He did Moses, then I have to stay! I have to be obedient! I have to do His will! Besides, this has been a pretty cool and awesome journey so far! No one will ever believe me when I tell them … "

Again, Elkan thinks about this new life and how he is leaving his old one behind. This is why he wants to go back, but he realizes he can't. He has to be like Moses. Elkan slips the stone into his ditty bag and leaps to his feet.

"Kamali! Captain Kamali!" Elkan yells as he runs, splashing through the water, back to Kamali. "You are right. I have to continue this journey. I will help you get that treasure to its rightful owner!"

"I am so happy to hear that, Elkan." Kamali replies grabbing Elkan's shoulders and giving a gentle fatherly shake. "I knew you would come to your senses. Besides, no one in their right mind would ever want to pass up the excitement and experiences that await you."

"Why was I chosen for this quest?

"Everyone is called, Elkan–but not everyone chooses to take the journey. You would have made the biggest mistake of your life if you had chosen not to continue the journey yourself."

Kamali then bends over, places his hands in the water,

scoops some up, and reaches his cupped hands toward Elkan. "Have you seen any of these yet?"

Elkan looks in Kamali's hands and sees a small fish in the cupped water. "It looks like a guppy!" Elkan exclaims.

"It is what you want to call it for it has no rightful name yet," Kamali replies.

Just then the fish jumps out of Kamali's hands and back into the ocean where a larger school of fish are waiting for its return. Once the fish rejoins the others, they swim out to deeper waters as a shelled creature passes beneath them and disappears as if it just turned invisible.

Curious, Elkan gets on his hands and knees and sticks his face into the water. As he opens his eyes he finds himself nose to nose with a sea snake. He quickly jumps up, turns to run and falls back down into the water. Kamali laughs heartily throwing his head and shoulders back then coming forward clapping his hands to his knees.

"Why such the rush? Are you late for something?"

"When I opened my eyes there was a sea snake right at my nose. I didn't want to get bitten."

"Now why would he do a thing like that? He was just as curious about you as you are about what things look like under the water. He wouldn't have harmed you Elkan. Remember, there is no death or suffering here."

"That's still not the easiest thing to get used to. I'm used to lots of death and suffering from many different things where I come from."

"Since you're already soaked and you know the sea animals won't hurt you, why don't you enjoy the perfect ocean and go for a swim?"

Without hesitation Elkan gets a big grin on his face, takes his shirt off, hobbles up to the shoreline one leg at a time as he takes his shoes off, throws his shirt and shoes onto the pebbled beach, and then splashes his way back into the water. When Elkan reaches waist high water he gives a little jump and dives in headfirst. When he opens his eyes again he sees a beautiful waterscape. The water is crystal clear. The floor of the ocean is covered with the same pebbles as the beach. There are lots of different kinds of fish and other sea creatures, many of which he has never seen before. He continues swimming out deeper.

He comes up for air and as he catches his breath he feels something touch his feet. Before he has a chance to look down, he is rising out of the water. Then he is suddenly thrust into the air and comes splashing back down. Once he has his wits about him again, Elkan looks around and doesn't see any-thing. He takes a deep breath, dives under the water and looks around. Again, he doesn't see anything that would have tossed him into the air.

What Elkan does notice is quite amazing. He sees very vibrant and beautiful coral all around. There are all different shades of red and blue and yellow, every color of the rainbow. Some of the coral is tubular and some is clustered. Some are large and some are small. There are sea urchins and other weird and wonderful creatures among the coral.

As Elkan looks around him, he sees millions of fish, sea serpents, sea reptiles and other types of sea creatures all around. He comes up for air and looks toward shore making sure he's not too far out to sea and that Kamali is still there. From the shore, Kamali signals to Elkan that he is keeping an eye on him.

Elkan takes another deep breath, dives under and paddles his way to the coral reef. A couple dolphin-like creatures swim up to Elkan and nudge his hand like a puppy wanting atten-tion. Elkan lifts his hand as the dolphin swims to position his hand on its dorsal fin and then starts to pull him along. When they bring Elkan up for air, he notices that he's by the ship. He looks up and sees the figurehead of the angel, again, looking beautiful and majestic.

He hears Kamali's voice from above, "Are you enjoying yourself? Do you want to come onboard?"

"Yes! I'm having a great time, but let me come up there for a rest."

Kamali leans over the bow of the ship and directs Elkan to the side where the dinghy is. There is a rope ladder there that Elkan climbs up.

As Elkan reaches the top of the ladder and steps onto the deck of the ship, he collapses, sprawling out. Kamali reaches out his hand to give Elkan a lift up.

"I see you met some of God's amazing creatures?" Kamali asks.

"Absolutely!" Elkan replies.

"Are you ready to head back to shore and make camp for the night?"

"Is it that time already?"

"Well, the sun is setting. That would mean that we do need to call it a day."

Elkan and Kamali get in the dinghy and head back to the shore. As they do, a very large sea lizard, about the size of a whale, swims beneath them. They get back to shore, set up camp and just as the sun is setting, see the large sea lizard off in the distance leap out of the water, spit fire and disappear back into the depths.

Elkan and Kamali rest their heads for the night as the sun sets, the moon glows, and the stars fill the sky with their twinkles.

"Achaia, let me sleep," Elkan mumbles as a cold nose nuzzles him awake. "Just lie down and let me sleep."

Elkan hears the continued rustling of footsteps and the

cold nose becomes hot breath on his face. Still half asleep, Elkan opens his eyes a crack expecting to see his dog.

"Ahhhhhh ... " Elkan screams, leaps to his feet and stumbles over them again, falling flat on his bottom.

Elkan's scream frightens his visitor, a small dinosaur, and it starts running in circles. Elkan gets back to his feet and the dinosaur runs straight at him. Elkan jumps up to avoid being hit as the dinosaur spins back around and catches Elkan's knees from behind. They both jump back up and run in circles again trying to avoid each other until the tent collapses on them. They both manage to find their way out of the tent at the same time and on the way out the dinosaur grabs one of Elkan's shoes. Elkan chases the dinosaur around the camp stumbling over his tent, the accoutrements, and even Kamali's tent. As Kamali rushes out of his tent the dinosaur runs off into the forest with Elkan's shoe in his mouth and a cup on his foot.

Kamali and Elkan both take off into the woods after the little dinosaur. They run down the path that grew up around them when they first arrived. The cup falls off the dinosaur's foot, but the little thief stays just far enough ahead that they can see him but can't catch up.

Just as they are about to give up, they enter a clearing. A large open field of green grass lies in front of them. In the center of the field is a large garden. They see the dinosaur heading toward the garden and they reengage in the chase. With their last surge of energy they reach the edge of the garden when they stumble over Elkan's shoe and land in the garden.

As they stand and brush off, they find themselves surrounded by animals - animals that are very strange, yet familiar to Elkan. There are animals similar to cattle, dogs, cats, lizards, deer, and dinosaurs just to name a few. They see their little thief and walk toward him. For the first time Elkan gets a good look at his mischievous little alarm clock. He stands about waist high. His skin is like that of a snake yet he stands on two larger powerful legs with two smaller ones like arms. He has a tail about the size of the rest of his body. His head is large with sharp teeth. His eyes are not cold like a snake or lizard, but much more inviting like a puppy dog. He sees Elkan and Kamali and cocks his head a little. It dawns on Elkan that his little thief looks similar to the pictures he's seen of T-Rex. *Maybe it is a baby T-Rex,* Elkan thinks to himself.

They see several trees throughout the garden, trees that are pleasing to the eye and good for food. But in the middle of the garden are two very different and unique trees. There is a river that runs next to them in the middle of the garden. They walk toward the river and trees and as they get closer, they notice the bark on the two trees is different from the others. The leaves are a different shape from the rest. They are even different from each other. Each one is unique and one-of-a-kind. The fruit on one tree is plain while the fruit on the other tree is like a cluster of grapes in a rainbow of colors.

About a stone's throw away they notice a man. He is a very well built man–a perfect specimen. He has brown hair and his skin is a medium brown.

"Who is that man and why is he naked?" Elkan asks Kamali.

Suddenly a loud, deep, commanding voice fills the air and vibrates in Elkan's chest. "You are free to eat from any tree in the garden; but you must not eat from the tree of the knowledge of good and evil, for when you eat of it you will surely die."

Kamali grabs Elkan and drags him to the ground. "Don't say a word!" Kamali whispers.

A few moments pass and Kamali lifts Elkan to his feet and grabs his arm. Kamali starts running back to the camp pulling

Elkan from the arm. When they reach the edge of the garden and enter the clearing again they stop.

"What was that all about?" asks Elkan.

"That man is Adam, the first man. We could not allow him to see and interact with us or we would alter history."

"What do you mean?"

"Do you know who Adam's wife is in the Bible?"

"Yeah, of course I do. It's Eve."

"Do you remember why Eve was created?"

"So that Adam could have a wife."

"Yes, but also so much more." Elkan and Kamali start walking the rest of the way back to camp as Kamali continues explaining. "We saw so many animals because Adam was naming them. The Bible tells us that after Adam was done naming the animals he saw that they all had others that were the same as them, but Adam had no one that was like him. He was alone and this is why Eve was created. Well that history is occurring right now. If Adam had seen us, he would have thought that there are others like him existing during his time and he would not have felt that he was alone. Therefore, Eve would never have come into existence; thus altering history forever. Remember, the Bible tells us that Adam was the first man, and thus the only man. We are not from this part of history but are experiencing it as if we were. It's being revealed to you Elkan. You need to experience it so that you know it is real and was real."

"So that was God's voice that we heard?"

"Of course!"

"So that means that when I first came on your ship the voice that said, 'let there be light' was God's also! He was the one that separated the waters!"

"Yes!"

"He was the one who brought forth the land and the sun

and moon and stars. He made the trees and plants grow up around us. He made the birds and the fish and the animals. We just missed Him actually forming Adam and breathing life into him! After each day the Bible tells us that what He did was good!"

"Exactly!"

"That is why the snake didn't bite me and whatever lifted me from the water didn't eat me or the little dinosaur didn't have me for breakfast. Everything was good! Everything is good! There was nothing bad. I think I get it! The pterodactyls are flying things so they were made with what I know as birds. The dinosaur is a land animal so it was made with the cows and dogs and other land animals. The Bible also tells us that all the creatures ate plants and that there was no death before Adam sinned!

"We need to get back to the garden! We need to stop Adam from eating the fruit!"

Kamali grabs Elkan by the arm and yanks him back.

"We can't! We can't alter what is going to happen! We have to continue on and not look back."

"But if we can stop it!" Elkan pleads.

"It is not up to us to stop it. That would place us at the level of God."

As they both continue back to the camp, Elkan is distraught. He knows what is about to happen.

As they arrive at the camp, Kamali tells Elkan to take a good look around. "Enjoy everything there is that God has created. It is good. It won't be like this forever. We need to stock up on food and water for the rest of our journey. We won't have another chance for some time. Let's get everything packed up and onto the ship, for tonight we sleep on board and tomorrow we rest."

As they are packing their gear, Elkan can't stop thinking

about what's going to happen. He wants in his heart to run back to the garden to stop it, but he knows in his mind that he isn't allowed.

Once everything is loaded onto the dinghy, Elkan takes a stroll along the beach one more time. He looks down at the rocks and the innumerable different varieties of colors and shapes. When he sees a flat one, he picks it up and skips it out to sea watching the ripples and counting how many times it hits. He watches the little fish swimming up to the edge of the water and then dashing back out as if they were playing chase. He listens to the songbirds singing in the trees with the occasional screech in the background to throw the song off key. He watches the occasional animal come to the water's edge for a drink, unafraid of his presence.

Why did God choose me for this journey? Elkan thinks to himself. *Why me? Who am I? I'm nobody special. I'm just a kid that lives ... lived in a small town. Why would he choose me for some great quest?*

Just then a rock at the water's edge catches his eye. It has gold flecks in it that catch the sun just right. The stone itself looks like a quartz stone. Elkan bends over to pick it up. As he lifts the stone it moves several others that it is partially buried beneath. A piece flakes off in his hand and when he pulls it from the water, he notices it's in the shape of a key. The part he saw glistening in the sun was only the part to hold onto. The key looks something like a small sword. It has a rounded handle about the size of a coin. The blade part is about finger length with a smaller bar crossing it near the tip. The handle has the gold flecks with beige swirls, while the blade has a crimson swirl included.

Elkan recognizes the shape on the handle as one that matches the shape on one of the locks on the chest. In absolute amazement Elkan screams out, "Kamali! Kamali!" He screams so loud and hard his voice cracks. "I found the key! I found the first key to unlock the chest!"

Elkan takes off running back toward Kamali grasping the key in his hand. "Look what I found," he continues yelling the entire way back.

As Elkan reaches Kamali he holds out his hand and opens it to show the stone key. "I found it!" Elkan pants. "I found the first key!"

"Let me take a look." Kamali calmly replies. "It certainly does look like a key. And it does have one of the symbols from the chest on the key."

Kamali turns the key in his hand studying it thoroughly. "Well, son, I think you're right. I would have to say that this most certainly appears to be a key. Put it in your ditty bag and let's head to the ship."

Kamali hands the quartz key back, and Elkan very carefully places it in his ditty bag. Then he secures the ditty bag extra tight so as not to lose it. They both climb into the dinghy and set off for the ship. Elkan looks back and ponders. Sadly he asks Kamali, "Will we ever go back there?"

Kamali gently replies, "No, Elkan. Tomorrow we rest, and then we set out to sea again. Don't look back at what was, keep your eyes on the ship's angel figurehead and think about what lies ahead. Where will it guide us next? Remember what you are learning and experiencing. Remember the truth so that one day you will be able to lead someone in the direction of truth."

Then Kamali mutters something else that makes no sense to Elkan. "Because that which may be known of God is manifest in them, for God has shown it to them."

"Elkan," Kamali states, "you are now without excuse."

Elkan sits with a puzzled look on his face as the dinghy arrives at the ship. They board the ship and unload the tremendous amount of food they brought with them from land. Once the food is stored, they drop barrel after barrel overboard to fill them with water. In all, they fill 40 barrels. Finally they head to the Captain's quarters for dinner. Elkan is anxious to try the key, but Kamali insists that he have patience.

Kamali turns his back and Elkan tries to sneak over to the chest to test the key. He pulls the key out and matches the symbol with that of the correct lock. Suddenly the key is pulled from his hand. As he turns, Kamali is standing behind him with a scowl, holding the key. Not a word is said, and they both head to the table to eat. Kamali places the key at the center of the table.

As they finish eating, Kamali slides the key across the heavy oak table and looks at Elkan. Elkan looks at the key and then back at him, and Kamali gives a nod. With the excitement of a child receiving presents on his birthday, Elkan jumps up from the table and runs over to the chest, places the key in the first lock of which the symbol matches and gives a turn.

Nothing!

The key doesn't turn.

"Is this the wrong key?" Elkan asks in a panic.

"Try again. This time line it up perfectly straight as you insert the key."

Elkan removes the key and inserts it again; this time he lines it up perfectly straight. As the key slides into the keyhole it goes in further this time. Elkan looks up at Kamali with wide-eyed excitement and bewilderment.

"The path is narrow," states Kamali. "The key wasn't going in as straight as an arrow the first time. Now, turn it."

Elkan turns the key, and the lock drops open.

"Now that you know the key works, close the lock and put the key back into your ditty bag," Kamali tells Elkan. "Keep it safe and secure."

Elkan does as he's told. He closes the lock, opens his ditty bag, places the key into it, and closes it again. He spends a few moments studying the chest then looks out the window to see the sun setting.

"I'm really exhausted," Elkan speaks into the air. "I'm going to head to my quarters and get some sleep."

"Very well!" Kamali replies. "Remember, tomorrow is a day of rest, and then we shove off to sea again."

As morning arrives, Elkan continues sleeping. When he finally awakes and starts above deck he hears Kamali from behind. "Ah, the boy finally meets the day!"

"I'm sorry, I guess I must have slept quite a while."

"No problem, my boy! This is the day of rest."

Elkan and Kamali reach the deck and the noontime sun shines down on the calm waters. The ocean is so smooth it looks like a blanket of silk in the reflection of the sun. Elkan looks overboard at the water and doesn't see a single fish. There's not a single bird in the sky as he looks off toward land. It is as though the entire world is at rest.

Elkan and Kamali spend the day talking about everything they have experienced the previous six days. Kamali tells Elkan that they will be setting sail before sun up. "If you would like to be there for the launch, let me know," Kamali tells him.

"Okay!" Elkan replies with excitement. "That would be pretty cool."

As the sun sets, they head to their quarters to get some rest.

Chapter 2

THE PENALTY

The brisk night air reminds Elkan of cool summer nights when he and his friends would play outside past sundown. A slight breeze gently rolls in from off the water and the moon is again large and bright—bright enough that he and Kamali don't need their lanterns to see.

Elkan and Kamali are at the bow of the ship watching the land slowly move off to the side when eventually the ship faces back out toward sea. A gust of wind fills the sails with a snap and carries them beyond the safety of the bay and out into the boundless sea.

"Where are we headed?" Elkan asks.

"Wherever *The Spirit* takes us, Elkan. You will find out when we get there," Kamali replies.

As Elkan sits on the deck staring at the night sky, he drifts off to sleep.

The sun rises over the horizon. The orange light reflects off the waves as they roll their way across the sea of gold—one disappearing as another appears. The early morning light wakes

Elkan. He stretches and rises to his feet. He sees Kamali at his usual place, the bow of the ship.

"Kamali," Elkan yells as he is taking off his shirt, "I'm going to take a quick dip in the sea to help me wake up!"

"No!" demands Kamali, "It is not safe."

"Why not, it was safe yesterday?" Elkan asks bewildered.

"That was yesterday! Today is different."

"How?"

"We are not in the place we were yesterday. Look out there." Kamali points to a bird resting on the water, bobbing up and down with the waves.

Suddenly a large sea creature rises out of the water with its mouth around the bird. Quicker than Elkan can blink his eyes or the bird can fly off, the jaws of the creature snap shut, leaving no sign of the bird. Then the creature returns to the depths of the sea.

Elkan stumbles back in horror.

"Let's go eat some breakfast," Kamali says as he wraps his arm around Elkan and they head to his quarters.

After breakfast Elkan walks over to the chest and stares at it. He rubs his hand over every groove and every embellishment like a blind man intensely studying an object.

Several days pass during which Elkan witnesses additional evidence that things are different than they used to be. He has seen dead fish, numerous fish and birds being eaten by other sea animals, and even a change in the seawater. When a wave splashes up and drops of water hit his face and lips it tastes different—not as pure—a little bit salty.

"Elkan!" yells Kamali. "Prepare for anchor. There is land up ahead."

Elkan runs to the bow of the ship and looks. Off in the distance land starts to appear. He sees a beach and trees but can't make out anything else. He also sees several birds ahead.

Several are floating and many more are flying around the same area. It looks like they are attacking something in the water. As the ship gets closer to the flock of birds, many of them fly off from fear of the ship being so close. Elkan looks closely at what the birds were making a ruckus about and sees the remains of what looks like a pterodactyl. The other birds were scavenging off of the remains of a sea attack.

A few moments later the ship stops. Kamali and Elkan gather their supplies, climb in the dinghy, and go ashore. Once on shore, Elkan quickly notices that things are totally different at this part of their journey than they were in the beginning. The beach is covered in seashells—some broken but most not. The majority of those that are broken have no more than a chip out of them. As they walk up the beach Elkan notices that the trees aren't as lush as the ones at the bay of the Sea of Creation. There is fruit on the ground rotting. He notices fewer flowers and the air doesn't smell as pleasant.

"Where are we Kamali?" Elkan asks.

"We are located somewhere in the Sea of Corruption," Kamali sadly replies.

The beach feels familiar to Elkan somehow. *Is it a beach from back home?* he wonders to himself. As he looks around he notices a path into the dense forest a little further up the beach.

"Let's check out the path," Elkan encourages Kamali as he runs toward it.

"We have a little time before we have to set up camp, so why not?" Kamali replies.

Elkan finds a stick on the ground that he uses for walking and to whack the brush as it gets in his way. As they head into the forest along the path, Elkan notices some craters in the ground. A closer look reveals that it's not a crater but a footprint—a footprint about twice the size of Elkan and several inches deep.

"We aren't going to run into any of the things that made these, are we?" Elkan questions pointing to the dozens of footprints trailing along the tree line.

"That I cannot promise," Kamali replies. "But rest assured you will know if we do!"

As they enter the forest along the path, Elkan notices that it is not as green and colorful as the previous forest. As they continue walking, Elkan uses his stick to push some bush branches out of his way. One of the branches releases from the stick sooner than Elkan anticipates.

With a sting, the branch whips his cheek and shoulder. Stumbling back in pain Elkan grabs his cheek and looks at his shoulder noticing a tear and a little blood where the branch had hit him. As he removes his hand from his cheek there is some blood on it also.

"Hold still, Elkan," commands Kamali as he reaches over and pulls a thorn out of Elkan's shoulder.

"Thorns?!" Elkan exclaims questionably dismayed. "There are thorns here!"

Kamali pulls up Elkan's sleeve and uses it to wipe away the blood. Then he takes a look around, walks a little off the path and into the forest and pulls a leaf off a plant. Stepping over other plants, he comes back to Elkan, reaches in his ditty bag and pulls out a small vial. He opens the vial and pours a little powder on the leaf and replaces the vial into his ditty bag. "Roll up your sleeve," Kamali orders Elkan. Elkan rolls up his sleeve and Kamali places the leaf, powder side down, onto the wound. "Hold this here," Kamali commands again. Then he walks over to a tall patch of grass about two feet high and pulls a couple blades from the ground, walks back to Elkan and uses them to tie the leaf onto Elkan's arm. "This will help keep it from festering."

"What was that you put on the leaf?" Elkan asks.

"Just a little remedy I carry with me," Kamali replies. "We probably ought to head back to the beach so we have time to set up camp."

So they turn around and head back along the trail to camp and turn in for the night.

The next day they head back along the trail, this time Elkan is prepared for the thorn bush. Along the way they watch a lizard scamper across the trail. Several hours pass as they weave their way along the path, through thick brush, fallen trees, and swarms of insects. The heat becomes unbearable, even under the protection of the forest. The ground is dry and hard. Elkan finds a log to sit on and rest. They both open their water bags, take a drink, and then wipe their brows.

There's a rustling in the brush behind where Elkan is sitting.

"Hold still," Kamali abruptly orders.

Leaves are moving behind Elkan.

"Hand me your walking stick, Elkan, but very slowly and quietly. Don't make any sudden movements or loud noises."

Elkan cautiously hands Kamali his walking stick. There is more rustling behind Elkan and more movement of the leaves.

From behind Elkan's right shoulder two eyes appear. Slowly a serpent's head rises up. Its eyes are a deep fiery orange with pitch-black slits for pupils. Its head is about the size of a baseball. Its scales are like jewels of all different colors that glitter in the rays of sun that penetrate the canopy above.

"Don't move whatever you do, Elkan," Kamali commands in a soft but firm voice. "And don't say a word. Don't even breathe."

Beads of sweat roll down Elkan's face from the heat, and now fear.

Kamali throws Elkan's walking stick down to the ground a couple feet away and no sooner does the stick hit the ground but the serpent springs over Elkan's shoulder and attacks the stick, wrapping itself around it and sinking its venomous fangs into the wood. Kamali approaches the snake, lifts his foot, and crushes its head with the heel of his boot. No sooner is the serpent's head a pulpy mass, and there is the sound of rustling leaves quickly rushing away from them into the forest.

"What j-j-just happened?" Elkan stutters.

"The enemy is aware of your quest now, Elkan. He has agents everywhere and they will do what they can to stop you on your journey."

"Enemy! You never told me anything about an enemy! You didn't tell me my life would be in danger! I'm supposed to trust you and you don't tell me I have an enemy!"

"Trust! Yes, trust! Have I not protected you, even just now? Have I not guided you and taught you along the way as a father would a son? Yes, you can trust me, Elkan. Remember, your success is dependent upon me, and it is my only desire to see you succeed!"

"You're right. I'm sorry. This whole serpent and enemy and enemy's agents thing just has me really psyched out."

Elkan looks down at his walking stick and the limp, dead snake wrapped around it. Insects have already started moving in to clean up the mess. Kamali and Elkan begin to walk again. Eventually they come to a clearing. It is a large field with a garden in the middle.

"That looks like the garden we were in before," exclaims Elkan, and he starts running toward it!

Kamali runs after Elkan. As they get closer Elkan stops in his tracks. He stares toward the garden as his jaw slowly drops open and his eyes squint, bringing his eyebrows toward each other.

"What is that?" Elkan asks bewildered.

Kamali continues walking toward the garden, so Elkan slowly follows behind.

Elkan sees two figures standing on each side of the entrance to the garden. They are like burning embers of coal, glowing and radiating like a flame. As they get closer to the garden, Elkan can finally make out the figures. They are strange creatures that he knows he has never seen before but something is telling him that he has. Each one is like a man. But each one has four faces. The main face is that of a man. On the right side is the face of a lion and on the left the face of a calf. The face on the back is that of an eagle. Each creature has four wings and two-toed hoofed feet like a calf–and they sparkle like burnished brass. From beneath the wings are hands like a man's. Each creature is facing the other, that is, the human faces are toward each other. Their wings are outstretched directly in front of them and are touching the wings of the other. There is lightning going forth from out of the figures.

Directly in front of the entrance to the garden and between the creatures and beneath their outstretched wings is a flaming sword. It is turning in every direction. Nothing visible is holding the sword and the movements are quick and swift and smooth. Like the appearance of a rainbow in a cloud on a rainy day, so was the appearance of the brightness all around it. Upon seeing this, Elkan fell to his face and wept without understanding why.

Elkan hears Kamali mutter another saying, "For the Word of God is living and powerful, and sharper than any two-edged sword."

Now Elkan and Kamali were approximately 100 feet from

the creatures and Kamali dropped to the ground next to Elkan. "Shhh! Don't make a sound," Kamali states.

Now a short distance away, while peaking over the tall grass, they see a man arriving with a woman, two male children, and a lamb. Before arriving at the entrance to the garden, the woman and children stop and fall to their faces. Elkan recognizes the man as Adam. He is clothed in sheepskin and carrying a young lamb. When Adam arrives at the entrance of the garden, he falls to his face for a moment, then rises and sacrifices the lamb.

Unable to bear the sight, Elkan buries his face into the ground and weeps some more.

As Adam leaves, Eve and the two boys join him as they head back into the forest.

Quickly, Elkan asks Kamali, "What was that all about?"

"Remember why you didn't want to leave the garden the first time we were here? You knew what was going to happen, but you couldn't interfere with God's plan. Adam and Eve ate from the Tree of the Knowledge of Good and Evil even though we heard God tell them not to–they disobeyed Him. Now, all of Creation has been corrupted by sin. Adam and Eve were driven from the garden. God placed the cherubim, the winged beings, here at the East entrance to the garden. The flaming sword shows the presence of a holy God and His word. The cherubim never leave the side of the Lord.

"So that's what those things are! Cherubim! I always thought they were pudgy little babies with wings."

"Certainly not! The cherubim are much more fantastic than what man's tiny little imaginations can conjure–and they are far from cute. Because of Adam's sin, death entered the world. God clothed Adam and Eve because they were embarrassed by their nakedness. In order to do this, God had to kill an innocent animal. Now, for payment of sin, God requires man to offer up sacrifices to Him. That is what Adam was doing—giving a sacrifice unto the Lord. In the presence of the Lord you can't help yourself but to fall to your face and praise Him and confess your sins. His glory is overwhelming, and He knows your heart."

"Why did He have to kick them out of the garden in the first place?" Elkan asks. "I understand they didn't obey God, but the damage was done—why kick them out?"

"Remember, Elkan, there is another tree in the garden—the Tree of Life. Now no one can eat of the Tree of Life. If God were to allow man to eat of the Tree of Life then man would live forever in sin. That is not God's will, and so God must protect it for the future when man will once again be able to eat of it."

"When will that be?"

"Not until the Lord renews this earth and comes to dwell with us in the new heaven and the new earth. For now, that is all I'm going to tell you about that. There is still much to learn before we address that topic." Kamali turns toward Elkan and looks him square in the eye and says, "You are like an infant; you can't be given meat when you can only handle milk."

Turning toward the path, Kamali suggests that they start back toward camp.

As they are talking along the way, they come upon the place where Kamali smote the serpent. Still wrapped around Elkan's walking stick, there isn't much left of the beast but bones and a little flesh. A couple of scavenger reptile-type creatures are still nibbling away as Elkan and Kamali stop and look down at it. They both glance up and scan the forest listening closely for any other danger in the area.

Elkan realizes it's not worth trying to salvage his stick and decides he'll have to find a new one.

There is a sudden fluttering in the trees as birds start

screaming. More rustling occurs along the ground as animals of all types peek their eyes over and through the brush and start to line up along the path. Elkan's heart jumps to his throat and starts pounding fast and hard. *Is another snake in the area?* he thinks to himself. *Are there more of the enemy's agents around?*

"Don't be afraid Elkan," Kamali suggests in a fatherly tone.

Just then Elkan sees a pure white animal coming toward them and hears the "baa" of a lamb. Elkan kneels down and puts his hand out toward the lamb as it comes nearer. There is not a sound in the forest—no birds squawking, no leaves rustling, not even a breeze blowing. The lamb approaches, looks at Elkan and continues along his way. He steps on the remains of the serpent as he passes, looks back at Elkan, looks down at the remains of the serpent and then turns to walk away. Elkan watches this in sheer amazement and curiosity. As the lamb disappears from sight, the birds in the trees and the creatures of the ground go about their routines and the forest returns to its previously busy state.

"Why isn't he with his flock?" Elkan asks bewildered. "Why is he here in the forest and not out in the field?"

"Maybe that is where he is headed. Maybe he has gone astray. Maybe he passed by here for a reason," Kamali answers as he looks down at where the lamb had trampled the serpent.

"Why did he purposefully walk on the bones of the snake when he could have easily walked around them?" Elkan continues as he himself looks down at the remains of the serpent wrapped around the walking stick that the lamb had walked upon. "And why did he seem to be telling me something by looking at me and then the serpent?"

Elkan no sooner gets the words out of his mouth when he notices the serpent's skull. The way the skull broke left a piece of it that looks something like a key.

"The key!" Elkan screams. "That's got to be the second key! Why else would the lamb seem to be trying to tell me something?" Elkan reaches down and grabs the bone fragment from the skull. He lifts it up to the rays of light coming through the canopy of the forest and examines it thoroughly. "It looks like a key alright—a skeleton key!"

Elkan places the key in his ditty bag and turns to Kamali and blurts out, "Let's get back to the ship so we can see if it works!"

Kamali smiles and agrees. About half way between where they found the key and the beach, the ground starts to rumble. Worried that an earthquake is starting, Elkan takes off running toward the beach so he can get off land and back to the ship. Kamali runs after him telling him to stop running.

As they get closer to the beach the rumbling gets louder and the earth shakes harder until finally Elkan loses his footing and goes flying face first into the ground just outside the edge of the forest. When Elkan lifts his head to regain his wits, he sees the absolute largest animal in the world.

"I have only seen those things as illustrations in books back home as something that is millions of years old."

In front of them is a herd of sauropod dinosaurs. The largest ones appear to reach to the clouds and stretch about as long as a football field from head to tail. The smallest ones are as small as a dog, and there is every size in-between.

"That my dear boy is a behemoth," replies Kamali. "'His bones are like beams of bronze, his ribs like bars of iron. He is first in the ways of God.' And no, they are not millions of years old. Think about it, just earlier today you saw Adam and Eve. They're not millions of years old. You know from the creation that these creatures were made on what day?"

"Day six," Elkan responds. "Day six, alongside of man. That's right, because that little dinosaur stole our stuff and we chased him into the forest. That is where we saw the garden for the first time—and Adam."

"You're catching on. Now look at behemoth, which God made along with man. Like I have told you many times before, remember what you are witnessing and hold it near and dear to your heart. It is all real and true."

"They don't even seem to notice us standing here," Elkan announces.

"They may not notice us, but we had certainly better notice them and where they are stepping," Kamali replies.

For the next couple hours they sit behind the brush and watch the herd slowly move on. Occasionally a couple of different types of dinosaurs, about the size of sheep or chickens, show up and pass the larger, slower ones.

The last of the herd passes as the sun is setting. Kamali and Elkan hurry back to their camp to make sure nothing was damaged. Fortunately, the camp was not in the path of the herd and was only knocked down and scattered about from the rumbling of the earth. They quickly set camp back up and crawl into their tents just as the sun transfers dominion of the sky over to the moon and stars.

The next morning, Elkan and Kamali rise up, pack their camping gear and load it onto the dinghy. Elkan wants to take one last stroll along the beach to collect a couple of shells. Kamali joins him as they walk the shell-covered beach in search of those special shells Elkan can take with him. While they are walking, a giant insect goes zooming by them. It looks kind of like a dragonfly, but it's almost as big as Elkan himself. Then, from way up in the sky they see a pterodactyl targeting the insect and zooming after it. Just as the pterodactyl gets close, the insect changes direction and the pterodactyl immediately adjusts its flight pattern to continue the chase. After several minutes of darting back and forth and dipping up and down, the giant insect meets its demise. It is no match for the long beak of the pterodactyl. After it catches the insect, it coasts over to one of the larger trees and perches on top while enjoying its breakfast.

Freaked out by the size of the insect and grossed out by the pterodactyl eating it, Elkan turns his attention to the shells again. He sees several different shapes, sizes and colors of shells, but the one thing that really captures his attention is how the insides of many of them reflect the sun in a pearl-like rainbow of different colors. He finds one that is about the size of a baseball and picks it up. As he looks at it and tilts it in the rays of the sun, the colors change. He tosses it back into the ocean and keeps looking for those one or two special shells. He eventually finds a small nautilus shell that is completely intact and a shell that has a design on it that looks like the flaming sword he saw at the garden. Satisfied, he places the shells into his ditty bag, looks over at Kamali and says, "Okay. Let's head back to the ship and try this key out."

Kamali nods his head, smiles, and says, "Let's do that ... but the last one back to the dinghy gets to row." And Kamali takes off running.

Elkan takes off running after him and yells, "No fair! You had a head start! I had no clue you were going to say that! I'm still going to beat you though!" And Elkan starts to gain ground on Kamali.

They arrive at the dinghy with Kamali one step ahead of Elkan. "I win!" Kamali exclaims.

"You had an unfair advantage since you called it before I had a chance to react," Elkan argues between panting breaths.

"You are right. I did have somewhat of an advantage, but I still won," Kamali rebuts. "Having knowledge does give one an unfair advantage over someone not knowing; the more you know, the less chance you have of someone taking advantage of you. Having said this, I would like you to learn how to row the dinghy. You can take us back to the ship."

Wide eyed and surprised, Elkan jumps into the dinghy and commands Kamali to get in. "We're heading back to the ship!"

Kamali laughs, gets in, and starts Elkan's lesson.

Once back on the ship, Elkan and Kamali unload the dinghy and head to the captain's quarters to try out the key. Elkan runs over to the chest, opens his ditty bag, pulls out the key and inserts it into the second lock—the plain one that is rusty and corroded. He turns the key and, just like the first lock, nothing happens. He looks at Kamali in bewilderment.

"Try unlocking them in order," Kamali suggests.

Elkan reaches into his ditty bag and pulls out the first key, the stone one. He inserts it carefully into the lock, remembering that it has to go in straight "for the road is narrow." He turns the key and the lock drops open. Then he focuses his attention on the second lock. Trying the key again, the lock squeaks as it unlocks and Elkan has to physically pull the lock down to open it.

"Remember," Kamali says in his fatherly tone, "the locks must be opened in sequence. Everything has its order, and God put that order into place for a reason. He didn't skip one single step in making His Creation. Nor did He skip a single step when He made you. Don't you try to skip a step when you are in His will, or you may just fall out of His will and into disaster! Now, secure the locks and put the keys away. Keep them safe and secure."

Elkan obeys and locks each lock back up placing the keys back into his ditty bag.

Meanwhile, Kamali is reaching into his safe and pulling out the old parchment map. He places it on the table, as he has done before, and unrolls it. He studies it. Elkan walks over to look at the map himself.

"Where are we on the map," Elkan asks?

Kamali continues studying the map and points to a place on the map within the Sea of Corruption. Elkan can see on the map every place they have been. From the beach at the Sea of Creation there is a trail on the map through a forest to an open area in which there is a picture of two trees—one looking like a vine full of fruit and the other like a typical fruit tree.

From the Sea of Corruption there is also a path through the forest into an open field, the same open field in which the same two trees are shown standing in the middle. He does notice though, that there is a small sword on the east side of the trees.

"I don't remember seeing that part of the map before when we looked at it," exclaims Elkan.

"You were not aware of the truth," Kamali replies. "Your eyes have been opened to the truth of that part of God's Creation and history so you are now able to see what is there."

"So where are we headed next," Elkan asks?

"Brace yourself, Elkan," Kamali says in a very somber and concerned voice. "Our next leg in the voyage is there," as he points to a place on the map called the Sea of Catastrophe!

Elkan looks at the map and sees different images in the Sea of Catastrophe. He sees swirls all throughout the sea, as well as the image of the wind blowing and lightning bolts.

CHAPTER 3

ONLY ONE

Late in the afternoon, as evening approaches, Kamali and Elkan set sail again. Several days pass at sea while Elkan learns more about *The Spirit of God* and sailing. He ventures into new parts of the ship and really begins to feel at home. He gets to know where everything is and what each part of the ship does.

After what seems like weeks or even months, Elkan is starting to get bored and frustrated that they haven't seen land and have been stuck on the ship. He starts wishing that he were back home in Arborstead with his friends and family. One day as he is eating some fruit and nuts and throwing the shells and pits overboard watching the fish and birds trying to eat them, Kamali approaches with a somber look on his face.

"Elkan," Kamali states with a firm voice and stiff jaw, "we must get prepared for some rough times."

"What do you mean 'rough times'?" questions Elkan.

"Severe weather will be here soon. Life and the world as we now know it will change forever."

"I thought it had already changed when Adam and Eve ate from the tree of the knowledge of good and evil?! The world then became dangerous with thorns and poison and animals that kill."

"Yes, Elkan, but there is more change to come. I want you to start staying close to me and do as I say without question or hesitation. If you do this, I will keep you safe."

With that, Kamali turns to leave and starts diligently scouring the ship for anything that is out of place or needs to be secured.

Elkan stands with a dumbfounded look on his face. He isn't quite sure what to think, and then he remembers the map. The next place they are headed is the Sea of Catastrophe. *With a name like that, nothing good could come out of it,* he thinks to himself.

A couple more days pass and on the morning of the third day, as Elkan is looking out over the ocean, he sees a huge wall of water burst forth from the sea for as far as he could see in each direction. It shoots high into the sky and then comes crashing down upon itself. A huge wave starts coming toward them, growing taller and more powerful as it gets closer. The same thing starts happening all around them. Steam starts rising from the ocean. Within a short time the sky turns dark. Strong winds start blowing. Elkan hears the sails of the ship snapping like a whip. Lightning stretches across the sky with its tentacles wiggling in every direction, occasionally tapping the ocean. Then, as if a faucet was turned on, the sky opens up and unloads a powerful rain down upon them. Kamali grabs Elkan by the arm and drags him toward the door that leads below deck. The waves slam into the ship and come crashing down over the entire deck, forcing Elkan out of Kamali's hands and thrusting him across the deck and into the side of the ship. The amount of rain and water makes it too hard for either to see the other. The sea is suddenly choppy and tossing the ship around, like a toy. The waves are huge and constantly pouring over the side of the ship, dragging Elkan from one part of the ship to another, mercilessly slamming him into everything in his path. Nothing can be heard except for the roaring of the waves and the pounding of the rain. The ship is tilting almost onto its side as it gets tossed around. As another wave washes Elkan across the ship's deck, Kamali is able to grab hold of his foot and drag him near. He helps Elkan to his feet, and they make a dash for the door to safety that leads below deck. As they head below deck, they see a flash of fire shooting from the ocean into the sky and then it is blocked out by another wave crashing down upon them, knocking them the rest of the way below deck.

Once below deck, Kamali tells Elkan to head to his quarters. Another wave comes pouring down the steps, knocking Kamali backward into the wall. He then stumbles up the steps as the ship is tilting back and forth, reaches for the door and gets slammed back down the steps from another wave. After several attempts, Kamali is finally able to pull the door shut.

Meanwhile Elkan stumbles, bouncing from wall to wall, to his quarters as Kamali had commanded. As he enters his room, he is smacked in the head by his hammock and then thrown back out into the hallway and then back into his room by the tossing of the ship. Seeing how even his hammock isn't safe, Elkan decides to brace himself in a corner, sitting on the floor with his legs bent but spread apart to counter any swaying as his hands brace each side.

A short while later Kamali enters Elkan's quarters.

"Follow me! We will go to my quarters where it is safer."

Elkan rises up with his arms out to each side ready to catch himself. He lumbers to the door and follows Kamali to the captain's quarters. Just as they reach Kamali's quarters, the ship is carried to the top of a wave and then dropped, thrusting Elkan ahead of Kamali and into the door headfirst. Elkan lies on the floor limp, his body rolling in whatever direction the ship is tossed. Kamali opens the door, picks him up, and carries him into the room.

Elkan's eyes open to find himself in the captain's quarters of the ship. Kamali is across the room at the table, examining the map. The ship is much calmer now and only gently rocking along the rolling waves.

"Is it over?" Elkan asks aloud.

"Yes, the storm is over," Kamali replies as he looks up from the map and over toward Elkan. "We will stay at sea for a little while longer which will give you plenty of time to rest and regain your strength."

Elkan reaches for his ditty bag.

"Oh no! I lost the bag! The ditty bag is gone! The keys! We'll never be able to open the chest without the keys! And the cargo inside will never make it to its rightful owner!"

"Don't worry, Elkan," Kamali replies as he walks over to the safe and draws out Elkan's ditty bag. "When you knocked your head, I took and placed the bag where I knew it wouldn't get lost."

"I thought you said you would protect me and keep me safe!" Elkan charges.

"You are alive aren't you? I didn't say I would keep you from getting some bumps and bruises, but I did keep you safe," Kamali responds.

"I want to go on deck to get some fresh air," Elkan states as he pulls himself together and heads to the door.

"Wait Elkan! I will go with you."

As soon as they go on deck Elkan gasps and chokes from the stench in the air. He is forced to cover his mouth and nose with his hand to try to cut down on the smell. There is steam rising from the water and clouds forming in the sky. The air is humid. Breezes blow across the water much more noticeably than before, enough to create white caps on the waves. The air is no longer still. As they look out from the bow of the ship, they see lots of debris floating in the water. And the water isn't even clear anymore. It is cloudy and muddy. Entire trees float by. There are no birds in the sky and not a speck of land to be seen. There are pieces of lava rock bobbing up and down in the waves, some as large as boulders. Carcasses of animals are floating throughout the sea. There are cattle and sheep and many different land animals, including some small dinosaurs; the sea animals have eaten parts of some. But amongst all of the destruction and ugliness a very large and vibrant rainbow appears in the sky off in the distance. Elkan is amazed that the sky is so beautiful when everything else is so disgusting.

"What about the ship," Elkan quickly turns to ask Kamali with his hand still over his nose and mouth?

"The ship is fine. It weathered the storm. As I said early on in this voyage, *The Spirit of God* is my fortress in which I put my trust. And we're about to put that trust into practice again! Look ahead Elkan!"

Elkan looks out ahead of the ship and sees a giant whirlpool straight ahead. Beyond that there are several other whirlpools lying in wait. "What do we do?" Elkan cries out.

"Nothing! It's too late to do anything under our power! Now, we just wait upon the Lord and His will! Pray, Elkan!"

Moments later they catch the outer rim of the whirlpool and it sucks the ship forward hard and fast. Just as they reach the backside of the whirlpool, it releases its grasp sending them on into the next one. Again, the outer rim of the whirlpool flings them along straight into the heart of another one. Trees hit the ship with a loud thump as they head deep into the heart of the whirlpool. Suddenly, the whirlpool vanishes before their eyes.

"Elkan, I'm not sure this next one will be so easy. Hold on!"

Just as Kamali says that, the whirlpool they are headed toward closes up and they sail on through.

Later in the day they come upon another series of whirlpools that fling the ship hard to the right and then suddenly hard to the left, thrusting them faster each time, like an out-of-control roller coaster. The ship creaks and pops as it is twisted in the two different directions. Once through, Elkan decides to go to his quarters, since he really doesn't feel well. He's dealing with his first case of true seasickness.

For the next few days Elkan stays below deck to regain his strength and avoid as much of the smell as possible.

After getting his rest, Elkan feels much better and makes his way to the deck. The ship is much smoother and only rocking a little. Once on deck, he sees Kamali at the bow with his scope up to his eye looking out over the water.

"Kamali," yells Elkan. "Are we there yet?"

"Almost," replies Kamali, "I think I see the summits of some mountains."

Elkan runs to the bow of the ship where Kamali is standing. "Let me see!"

Kamali hands Elkan the telescope and points him in the direction of the mountain summits. "By evening we should be close enough to set anchor."

For the next couple hours Elkan and Kamali stand at the bow of the ship talking and enjoying the breeze. The stench isn't nearly as bad as it was. The breeze helps to keep it fresh. And the water is much clearer and looks more like an ocean now. Shortly after mid-afternoon, they head to the captain's quarters for something to eat.

"Why is there so much bad stuff happening?" Elkan inquires.

As they walk toward the cabin, Kamali places his arm around Elkan's shoulders and explains, "Well, Elkan, it goes back to the garden. Remember when Adam ate the fruit? That was a sin against God and from then forward all the Creation groans and suffers in pain together. Since that moment the wickedness of man has been great upon the earth, and God judges man according to his heart. You may know of the place we are headed, but I will not tell you until we are there for fear that it might corrupt your senses and blind you to the truth."

They enter the cabin and enjoy their meal. Elkan looks over at the chest as his mind wonders about what might be in it and where he will find each key and what the keys will look like, as each one is different so far. He finishes his meal and gets up from the table and heads to the chest. He looks over the chest again, studying the third lock, the one for which he hopes he will find the next key. The bronze lock is heavy in his hand and the engraving of the seven half circles inside of each other is well worn, but visible. He looks at the back of the lock and sees another engraving. It is in a language Elkan doesn't understand, so he asks Kamali if he knows what it says.

"It is in the original language and says 'only one man, righteous,'" Kamali recites from across the room.

"I take it you've read it before?"

"Many, many times Elkan. More than you can imagine"

"So you probably know every little detail of these locks and the chest?'

"Yes, as well as the one who has created them."

Elkan looks up at Kamali questioningly as Kamali looks back with an all-knowing grin, as if he knows something no one else does.

Kamali motions for Elkan to go with him as they head to

the part of the ship where the food and water is stored. They count the barrels of water and the sacks of food.

"It appears we have plenty of water for the voyage, but we will need to get more food before too long," Kamali states. "Now, we must go and prepare to set anchor before the sun sets."

They head back to the bow of the ship and see the mountain range much closer now and land a short distance away. They anchor ship and then watch the light on the mountains from the reflection of the setting sun behind them. As the last of the sunlight vanishes from the tips of the mountains they head below to their rooms to get some sleep.

After what seems like only minutes, Elkan hears knocking on his door. It's Kamali.

"Elkan, get up! It's time to start the day!" Kamali continues pounding on the door.

Elkan stumbles out of his hammock and to the door. He lifts the latch and opens it to Kamali's face reflecting in the light of a lantern.

"What time is it?" Elkan asks with a groggy, still half asleep, voice. "Is the sun even up yet?"

"We don't have time for that. We must get started by daybreak! Here, put this on." Kamali hands him a pile of woolen clothes.

Elkan closes the door, changes into the new clothes—sandals and a scratchy woolen tunic and cloth strip for a belt. Then he opens the door again just to have Kamali grab him by the shoulder and drag him up onto the deck of the ship. Slowly waking up, Elkan helps Kamali load the dinghy and push off toward shore. Along the way, they see a glow come from around the mountains as the sky starts to light up. Between two peaks, they see the bright orange ball of the sun slowly rise to meet the morning. Elkan notices that Kamali isn't in his regular captain's garb either but also wearing a tunic and sandals.

"Why are we dressed like this?"

"So that we may blend in with the people we will meet."

They reach shore and pull the boat up through the reeds onto dry land. They grab their water bags, and Elkan double checks to make sure he has his ditty bag securely at his side.

As they wander along the shore they come upon a stream that is coming from the direction of the mountains. They follow it for a little while until they come upon a woman gathering water into her pitcher from the stream. Kamali instructs Elkan not to say anything and let him do the talking.

Kamali goes to meet her and says something in a different language. She offers him some water and he drinks. They talk a little more and then Kamali motions to Elkan to follow. They journey into the mountains and Elkan whispers to Kamali so the woman doesn't hear, "What did you say to her? What language was that? How am I supposed to fit in if I don't know the language?"

"I asked her for a drink of water so she gave me some. I gave her ten shekels and asked her whose daughter she is and if there is room in her father's house for us to stay for the night. She told me her father is Arphaxad, son of Shem, and that they have enough of both straw and food and room for lodging."

"There is one original language, Elkan, the one you saw on the lock on the chest. Everyone speaks that language. You must listen with your heart, as well as your ears, to know it. Don't think about what you don't understand, but understand what you don't know. That is the beginning of wisdom, and with wisdom you will know and understand."

Totally confused with what Kamali just said, Elkan tries to listen and understand, without success, some of what Kamali and the woman are talking about.

They arrive at a camp and go directly into a tent. There is a man there with his wife and several children. Entering the tent behind them is another man. The woman from the stream says something to the first man and Kamali kneels down before him. Elkan follows suit and does the same. Kamali is introduced to the other man who walked in behind them and again he bows down before him. Elkan repeats the same.

They all sit on the dirt floor of the tent and start talking. The surrounding commotion becomes a blur of noise to Elkan as he is concentrating on what they might be saying. Elkan says a quick prayer for understanding when suddenly his ears pop. He grabs his ears with his hands from the sharp pain and notices everyone looking at him. As he lowers his hands, he hears everyone talking to him and actually understands them as they ask him if he is well. Without thinking about not knowing the language he replies that he is fine, and everyone understands him. From that point on, he can understand and follow the conversation that is going on in the tent. He learns that the owner of the tent, the first man they met, is Arphaxad and the second man they met is named Selah, Arphaxad's son.

Arphaxad tells them the story of how his family came to be in this place. He tells of his father, Shem, and his father's father, Noah. He tells of a judgment of all of mankind because of their wickedness and evil. There was one man, though, his grandfather, Noah, who found favor in the Lord's eyes for his righteousness. The Lord told him to make an ark because He was going to destroy every living thing with a flood. Only Noah and his wife and his sons and their wives were on the ark to be saved from God's fury, one of those sons being Arphaxad's father Shem. Arphaxad's uncles, Shem's brothers, are named Japheth and Ham. They live in another part of the camp, as does Noah himself. Kamali talks to them as if he knows the history as well as them. As Elkan and Kamali's hosts recount the story, they discuss taking a journey back to the ark's resting place. With that, Elkan's ears really perk up and the excitement jolts through his veins just thinking about seeing this historic ship that has been all but explained away as simply a legend.

Arphaxad tells Anke, the daughter who brought Elkan and Kamali to the tent, to go prepare a lamb for a feast tonight. So she leaves the tent obediently. Arphaxad's wife then gets up, gathers the children, and leaves also to go help prepare the meal.

With the women and children gone, Arphaxad, Selah, Kamali, and Elkan continue talking. Arphaxad asks Kamali and Elkan if they would like to see the ark. "Even though it has been nearly 100 years since the flood waters were drawn back, the ark is still in its very same resting place," he says.

"One day the ark will be gone and no longer a reminder," says Arphaxad, "but God gave us an everlasting sign of His covenant with us—the rainbow. God's covenant says that He will never flood the earth and destroy every living thing on it again."

"I've heard that!" shouts Elkan with excitement.

"I would hope so. Everyone knows God's covenant as well as His word," replies Selah.

Moments later it is time for the festivities, and they all leave the tent to eat and celebrate. Late into the night Elkan and Kamali are shown where they will sleep. It is a tent with beds of straw. As soon as Elkan sees his bed he thinks to himself, "Wow! I am going to be much more thankful for my hammock after sleeping in this."

Elkan and Kamali say good night and fall asleep to the chirping insects and the occasional neigh, baa or grunt of goats, sheep, and camels.

The morning sun awakens Elkan with new excitement.

He knows he's going to see Noah's Ark–the real, honest to goodness, actual, authentic, only one of its kind, never duplicated, exactly as it says in history, true ark. He jumps up out of his straw bed, runs down to the river to freshen up and almost falls in the water with laughter when he sees his reflection. His hair is messy and tangled, but even worse is that he has straw sticking out everywhere. He sticks his entire head in the water and then combs his fingers through his hair to get the straw out. Once cleaned up, he runs back to camp to make sure everyone else is up and ready to go see the ark.

When Elkan returns everyone is looking at him. Suddenly they start laughing.

"What's so funny?" Elkan asks.

"I guess you didn't realize it," Kamali explains, "but we were already up when you came running out of the tent with your hair full of straw. You looked like you just sat on hot coals and had to get to the river to put the fire out."

Embarrassed, Elkan has no choice but to laugh at himself, just imagining what he must have looked like. After the laughter dies down, Elkan pushes to leave now to go see the ark.

"Grab something to eat," Arphaxad tells him. "We will have to prepare as it is a day's journey there and back."

Once packed, they head along paths up the side of the mountain. Early in the afternoon they arrive at a place where they can see the ark resting gently on a plateau. It's nothing like Elkan had expected–nothing like the pictures he has seen. It is very, very large.

"How big is that thing?" Elkan gasps with an open jaw.

"It is precisely three hundred cubits long, fifty cubits wide, and thirty cubits high," replies Arphaxad. "The exact size God told Noah to make it."

As they get closer Elkan notices it is a black brown color. There is a large door that is open like a ramp, as well as a single small window at the top. It is rather box-like and simple. As they approach, Elkan realizes the true magnitude of the ark. It is about three football fields long and about four stories high. There are a few vines growing up it. Trees are growing around it. Grass and small shrubs are growing in a couple of places on top. There is an occasional mouse that scurries across the ramp and into the ark that reminds Elkan of the ones that make his church their home. A hawk flies overhead and lands on the top of a tall tree. The sky is blue with puffy white clouds decorating it.

They step up onto the ramp door and start walking in. Elkan is amazed at how tightly fit the boards are.

"The Lord told Noah to seal the ark both inside and out with pitch," comments Arphaxad.

"And once all the animals and Noah's family were in, Noah closed this very door that we are standing on and the Lord sealed it shut," continues Selah.

"How did Noah get all the animals on the ark?" asks Elkan.

"What do you mean?" Arphaxad counters.

"With all the animals in the world, how did he get them all on the ark; and two of each at that?"

"How quickly history is lost, and it only takes a couple generations," Arphaxad sighs. "There aren't that many different kinds of animals in the world and God told Noah that he only needed two of each KIND of unclean animal, male and female, and seven pairs of each KIND of clean animal, male and female. Also, he didn't need to bring on the water creatures, only those that move upon the earth and take to the sky."

"In other words, Elkan," Kamali continues, "Noah only needed one pair of the horse kind and one pair of the dog kind being unclean and seven pairs of the sheep kind being that they are clean … He didn't need every different breed of each animal."

"Let's continue on into the ark," Selah suggests.

As they walk up the mossy ramp and into the ark, it is dark. Arphaxad and Selah both light torches as they enter. Elkan watches the heat and flame from the torches touch some spider webs and make them curl up and disappear. The moss under Elkan's sandals feels squishy like a thin sponge. It smells musty and damp, like it does deep in the forest. The outside wood still appears well preserved, but some of the wood on the inside is decaying.

"This is the lower of three levels," Arphaxad explains. "This is where all of the larger animals were; the camels, the hippos, the elephants, and some of the kinds of dragons."

Elkan remembers the beach. What Kamali called dragons, he knows as dinosaurs.

"Most were younger which made them smaller, easier to handle and also when they got off the ark they were able to do as God said and be fruitful and multiply," Arphaxad continues.

Elkan sees the stalls where the animals were kept. He also notices the trough where the animal waste would have been scooped to and dealt with. After walking the entire distance of the ark to the far end, he notices that to go to the next level there is a ramp, not stairs or a ladder, as he would have thought. *I guess that makes sense,* he thinks to himself. *Noah couldn't have carried the animals up stairs or ladders to get them to the upper levels so he built ramps.*

As they continue up the ramp to the second level Arphaxad explains, "This level is where the medium sized animals would have been kept, like horses and deer and animals that size. Things certainly changed because of the flood. God said that every beast of the earth and every bird of the air would fear and dread man, as well as every fish in the sea. He also said that every moving thing that lives would be food, just as He gave us the green herbs. The one stipulation is that we are not to eat meat with blood, because it contains life."

As they continue down the corridor, Elkan notices many different insects flying and crawling around as well as a big furry caterpillar inching along a rail. A lizard scampers across the walkway and up a pole, stops, looks around and then continues into the rafters.

Thinking about what was just said, Elkan wonders aloud, "So Noah and everyone before the flood only ate fruits and vegetables?"

"As well as nuts," Selah adds.

"Although some ate meat at that time because they were disobeying God," continued Arphaxad. "Noah and his family where righteous and did not eat meat. But again, God told us it is okay now."

Arphaxad and Selah show Elkan and Kamali where the food was stored, how the animals were fed and taken care of, even how they gathered the water from the rain.

"How long was everyone on the ark?" Elkan asks.

"Just over a year," Arphaxad replies, "One year and ten days to be exact."

The third and upper level, it was explained, was where the smallest of animals were kept; the birds, rabbits and even the mice. After they had toured the three levels, Arphaxad and Selah show them a small area at the top of a ladder just large enough for them to get their upper bodies into while standing on the ladder.

"This is the window from which Noah sent forth the raven and then later the dove," explains Arphaxad. "This is also the window through which he saw that the rain had stopped and first saw the tops of the mountains."

Amazed at the view, Elkan pulls himself up off the ladder and pushes through the window onto the roof of the ark. As he stands there looking around, he has a whole new perspective of the world. Not too far into the distance, a little further up the mountain, he sees a couple of pterodactyls circling around just below the snow-capped peak. Way off in the other direction, he sees the ocean and *The Spirit of God* peacefully resting on the waters. A short distance from the ark, Elkan sees something he didn't see before; a pile of stones with some overgrowth that look as if they were piled up on purpose.

"What is that pile of stones over there?" Elkan asks as he leans over toward the window and points.

"When Jehovah–God told Noah to leave the ark, he built an altar to the Lord. Then he offered burnt offerings on the altar of every clean animal and every clean bird," replies Arphaxad. "That is the altar Noah built!"

Elkan stands in awe of everything he sees and reflects on what he has been learning, picturing in his mind what it would have been like to be on the ark or to have been left behind because you didn't believe Noah, shrugging him off as a crazy man. A breeze blows across the mountainside as the tree branches bow and the leaves rustle.

So, as far as I can see, including the mountain top behind me, was completely covered in water. This very ark was the salvation of only a few people as a result of one man's righteousness. How quickly death would have come to those who didn't believe God's word once the waters rushed in, more quickly and more powerfully than a hurricane. Something like what I witnessed on The Spirit of God not too long ago? Elkan ponders.

Elkan walks to the edge of the roof and looks down. He sees the ramp door by which they entered, covered with bits of moss and dirt. As large as the door is, it looks much smaller from this vantage point. Realizing the danger if he was to slip and fall over the edge, Elkan decides to head back to the window, taking one last look around at the world before crawling back in.

Once down the ladder, Selah mentions the position of the sun in the sky and that they need to get back to camp before it gets too late.

Arphaxad and Kamali agree, and they head back to the lowest level of the ark to leave. Elkan is quiet, still pondering everything and looking around at every little detail he can see. As they reach the door Arphaxad stops and explains that when all of the animals and Noah and his family were on board, Jehovah shut the door and sealed it behind them. When the ark came to a rest, Noah and his family removed the pitch covering from around the door to open it. Then they took this key, he points to a brass key hanging on a hook, and unlocked all of the stalls setting the animals free.

"Key?" Elkan perks up and shouts. "Could this be the key we need, Kamali?"

"You tell me."

"I think it is!" Elkan looks to Arphaxad and asks, "May we have that key?"

"I don't see why not. Not many people come here anymore and there is certainly no need for the key."

Elkan thanks him excitedly and reaches up to take the key off the hook. He runs out of the ark and jumps part of the way off the ramp. "Com'on Kamali! We gotta get back to the ship. We need to try this key to see if it's the one. The lock has seven half circles inside each other; this has to be the rainbow of God's promise. And the writing that says, 'one man, righteous'; this can only be referring to Noah! I just know this is the key!"

"Patience, Elkan! We have time to get back. We must be

respectful of our host's hospitality. We will stay tonight and leave in the morning."

Heartbroken and impatient, Elkan places the key into his ditty bag and stomps off down the path back toward camp.

The evening passes with dinner and more discussion before turning in. Elkan periodically looks in his ditty bag and plays with the keys, looking at all of them together and then puts them back.

As the morning comes, Elkan is quick to rise and wakes Kamali, rushing him to get up so they can get back to the ship.

The rest of the camp is rising and starting their day. Elkan and Kamali prepare for their journey back to the ship, thanking Arphaxad and Selah for their hospitality. With a shake and a hug, Elkan and Kamali are on their way to return to *The Spirit of God*.

Once back on the ship, Elkan rushes to Kamali's quarters to try out the key. He runs to the end of the corridor opening his ditty bag and grabbing the brass key. Kamali unlocks the door to the captain's quarters, and Elkan throws it open. Stumbling to the chest he grabs the third lock, the one with the seven half circles, the rainbow. Fumbling around with the lock trying to get a good handle of it, he sticks the key in when he hears Kamali call his name in a bold voice, "Elkan!"

Elkan stops and looks back.

"Don't forget that you must open the locks in sequence!"

"Oh yeah!" So Elkan pulls all of the keys out of his bag, places each one into its respective lock, and unlocks them one at a time until he gets to the third and newest lock. He turns the key, hears a click, gives the lock a tug, and it opens.

"Yes!" Elkan exclaims as he jumps up, throws his arms open, looks up and then drops his head down pumping his fists. Then he dances around like a crazy man with his arms out.

Kamali just stands in the corner of the room laughing.

When Elkan finishes his antics, he and Kamali remove the map from the safe and roll it out on the table just as before. This time as the map is rolled out to the Sea of Catastrophe, Elkan sees an image of the ark with a rainbow arching over it. He sees the images of eight people, four men and four women, as well as a line of animals leaving the ark and spreading out across the map.

"So," begins Elkan, "Noah and Moses are similar; they were both chosen by God. But they are different in that Noah listened to God and did as He said, whereas Moses argued at first but then listened. In the end though, they were both obedient and God used them to preserve His people."

"Yes, you could look at it that way, Elkan" replies Kamali.

Again, Elkan looks at the map to see what lies ahead, and again, he only sees the name of the next sea they are to journey through—the Sea of Confusion.

For the rest of the evening, before turning in for the night, Elkan and Kamali sit at the table eating dinner and discussing what Elkan had learned throughout this leg of the journey. Kamali explains to Elkan that he must continue wearing these clothes because they will continue to meet people throughout the rest of the journey, and they must be able to fit in.

Chapter 4

DIVIDED

The next morning Elkan awakes to discover that the ship is already pursuing its next course. He also discovers that there is a heavy fog over the ocean. He can't see five feet in front of him.

"You can almost cut it with a knife, can't you?" he hears Kamali's voice from somewhere off to the side.

"Where are you? I can't see a thing!"

"Follow my voice Elkan. Where will you always find me?"

"The bow of the ship! You are always at the bow of the ship looking off in the distance."

Elkan starts walking toward the bow of the ship watching very closely what lies ahead so he doesn't trip over or run into anything.

"Yes, but this time my looking glass is of no use. It doesn't allow me to see through this heavy mist."

Like a ghostly figure, Kamali appears as Elkan approaches the bow.

"How do you know where we are going then?" Elkan asks as he reaches Kamali's side.

"*The Spirit of God* will always lead us in the right direction. Just have faith and trust."

"You always talk as if this ship is human or has some magical powers or something."

"No Elkan. *The Spirit of God* is not human nor is it magical, but I do always trust *The Spirit* to carry me through times of trouble, as well as times of smooth sailing."

"Well, then you have more faith than I do, but if you trust it, I trust you!"

"We do not always know where *The Spirit* will lead, but if we trust it, we will get to where it takes us. Whenever *The Spirit* moves we have to prepare ourselves for a journey, not always knowing where we will end up. If we knew, then part of the excitement would be gone."

Elkan nods his head in agreement. "But don't you get scared of what's ahead?"

"No, because I always have an angel before me to keep me in the way and to bring me into the place which has been prepared," Kamali says as he points down toward the figurehead of the ship.

"Sometimes I don't completely understand you, Kamali."

"I don't always expect you to. You can't always rely on your own understanding. If you did, you wouldn't have made it this far into the journey. That is why you need faith, to carry you through those times of confusion."

Elkan walks back to mid-ship, strategically maneuvering through the fog and around the ship's obstacles. It's quiet aside from the creaking of the ship and the rolling of the waves.

Kamali yells back to him, "Meet me in my quarters. I will be down momentarily."

"Okay." Elkan responds as he reaches down to open the hatch.

Elkan waits for Kamali in his quarters for only a few minutes when Kamali opens the door and declares, "You're going to learn a new culture!"

"What?"

"A new culture! You had a crash course in the culture of Noah's descendents, but now I'm going to teach you everything you need to know about how to fit into the culture."

"But why? We aren't there anymore!"

"No, we aren't, but we will be interacting with the culture again and you must be prepared in order to succeed at your quest. Now, have a seat … "

Elkan sits and spends the next couple days learning about the original Hebrew culture, periodically taking breaks to go above deck to check their progress. They cover everything from his clothing to manners and food to rituals. Elkan is totally submersed into learning this new culture.

On the third day, they break from learning and go above deck. The fog is thinner than it was before and Kamali navigates his way to the bow of the ship with Elkan on his heels.

Kamali lifts up his scope and looks out into the distance.

"Still foggy but I can see an outline of land some distance up ahead."

"Let me see!"

Kamali hands the scope to Elkan and points him in the right direction.

"I don't see anything but fog."

"Because your eyes are not yet trained to see the truth, the absolute truth."

"What do you mean?" Elkan asks, handing the scope back to Kamali. "I see what I see and that's truth!"

"Not quite Elkan. You are still learning to see the absolute truth, but don't worry, you'll get there if you keep trying and practicing."

"Then teach me. You've been teaching me all of this other stuff; teach me to see the absolute truth."

"That is not something that can be taught, Elkan. You must learn not to see through your own eyes, but through the eyes of the One who made everything."

"How am I supposed to see through His eyes when He is God and I am not? He sees all things, but I can only see what's around me. My truth is what I know—what I see and experience! I can't know all things the way He does!"

"As I said before, don't lean on your own understanding."

And with that, Elkan plops down next to the main mast and sits with his back against it.

A short while later the light grows dim as the sun sets, even though they can't see the sun itself through the dense fog. Kamali lights his lantern, and Elkan can slightly see it through the fog. Suddenly, like stepping into another world, the fog lifts and Elkan sees Kamali's lantern clearly. The moon offers just enough light to see the outline of the ship as Elkan lifts himself to his feet and cautiously runs back to the bow where Kamali still stands.

"Look!"

Elkan looks in the direction Kamali is pointing and he sees a slight glow in the distance.

"What is it?"

"Civilization."

"You mean a city?"

"Yes, but not like what you're thinking."

"A city's a city!"

"But this city is not like what you have pictured in your mind. You have not seen a city like this before."

"You've been here before?"

"Yes, I have sailed the world Elkan. There is not a drop of water this ship has not moved upon. There is not a creature that breathes on the face of the earth that I don't know of. Yes, I know this city, and I know it well. And I know what the people of the city are like."

"What are they like?"

"You will soon find out for yourself. Stay near me when we get there. It won't be until morning so let us get some sleep."

Elkan and Kamali head to their quarters to get some sleep.

As the day breaks and the sun rises, Elkan and Kamali, dressed in their tunics and sandals, head above deck. Welcoming them in the distance is a tall tower that reaches above the hills and trees and on into the sky. The rising morning mist covers the top of the tower.

"Wow! What's that?" Elkan asks in amazement.

"That is where we are headed," Kamali states as they stand at the bow of the ship and look through Kamali's scope. "Would you like to see it up close?"

"Well, yeah!"

Elkan looks through Kamali's scope and sees people working on the tower, maneuvering large blocks up the side and toward the top. The blocks are bigger than any of the men.

"That's not what I mean by closer, Elkan. Would you like to go visit it?"

Elkan turns on his heels to face Kamali. "Can we?"

"That is why we are here. Let's prepare the dinghy to go ashore."

Elkan and Kamali prepare the dinghy and head to shore. They row toward the mouth of a river spilling into the sea. Rowing becomes a challenge as they begin to feel the current working against them.

"Why are we going toward the mouth of the river?" asks Elkan.

"We need to get up stream a little for an easier journey to the city," Kamali replies.

They finally make it through the force of the current flowing from the mouth of the river. Although still difficult, rowing does become a little easier.

A few moments later, long after the sea is out of view, they begin seeing people, especially women, by the edge of the water. Many of them gathering water in their pitchers, while others are leading their sheep and goats to drink. Everyone is dressed similarly to Arphaxad's family except the women have more jewelry and makeup on.

Elkan and Kamali come upon an area where they can steer their boat ashore. Elkan notices that not many people are paying attention to them. They are all busy going about their daily routines.

As they climb out of the dinghy, Elkan ties it to a nearby tree while Kamali walks off and begins talking to one of the locals. They are just out of hearing range for Elkan to know what they are talking about, but the man points with his staff toward a dirt road where many people are coming and going. Once the dinghy is secured, Elkan catches up with Kamali.

"That is the road we take to the city," states Kamali.

"What city is it?"

"It is called Bab-ilu. We will go there in search of a man named Eber."

"Who is this, Eber?"

"One who can teach us about the city and the tower that you saw from the ship."

Elkan and Kamali head down the road toward the city, passing many people along the way. Occasionally there is a shepherd with his flock taking up the entire road, and everyone just has to walk through or around the flock. As they walk through the flock, Elkan can smell them, reminding him of a petting zoo. As he gets near them, they try to run out of the way but can't because of the sheep in front. This allows Elkan to touch their thick, curly fur.

There are also merchants selling things like jewelry, vegetables and little golden idols of cows and birds, lions with a man's head and other strange creatures along the road. Some have roadside stands, while others walk the road with their goods. Throughout the day Elkan and Kamali purchase food like fish, bread, and fruit from some of the merchants.

By evening they arrive at the outskirts of the city. To Elkan's amazement, it looks like a city in what he knows as modern-day Israel from pictures he has seen. The houses are made of clay with doors and windows and some even have a second level. There are people on the roofs of the houses placing large clay pots in particular places. He also sees children playing games and women preparing grains and placing them in the clay pots.

The city is large with streets going here and there and crossing each other—and there, in the near distance, is the tower reaching toward the clouds. *It is so enormous you can fit another city inside of it,* \ Elkan thinks to himself in awe. Kamali asks a man passing by where an inn might be. Replying, the man points down one of the streets and then points in one direction and then another about three or four times before he departs. Kamali motions for Elkan, and they start down the first street turning down a few others, with each one getting narrower, until they arrive at the inn.

Kamali knocks on the door and a man opens it. Kamali inquires about a room and the man smiles, tells Kamali the price and then welcomes them in. Elkan notices that the furnishings are quite simple. Everything is made of wood or clay, and he does not see any pictures on the wall.

Reaching into his bag, Kamali pulls out some money and pays the man who then shows them to their room. They head back out the door and around to the side and up some steps. The man opens a door and leads them in.

"This is your room. I pray you have a restful night," the innkeeper says as he lights a lantern and leaves the room, closing the door behind him.

The sun is dropping fast and Elkan surveys the room. There is simply a lantern, two mats on the floor with wool blankets, a clay washbasin, and built-in clay benches by a single window.

"Certainly nothing fancy about this place!" Elkan remarks. "No pool. No room service. No television. What kind of five star hotel is this?" he continues jokingly.

"We don't need it. It serves our purpose for sleep. We could have very easily been sleeping in an alley where it isn't safe. Now let's get some rest."

With that, they lie down, close their eyes, and go to sleep.

During the night Elkan dreams of serpents chasing him. They are right on his heels, and one is even able to bite his heel leaving a small cut. Just as they are about to overtake him, a bright, blinding light appears before him and the serpents stop - rearing up hissing and spitting and saying things in strange languages. Elkan runs into the light. There he sees a golden key floating before him. He grabs it and when he looks down at it he sees a book with no title. As he opens the book, he wakes up.

Distressed over his dream, Elkan looks over to Kamali to see if he's awake so he can tell him. Kamali is not there so Elkan panics and jumps to his feet with his heart pounding to find him. Immediately, a sharp pain shoots through his heel and he cries out and falls back to the floor. He looks at his throbbing heel and notices a cut on it.

From a dark corner of the room he hears Kamali's voice, "You can't out-run your past Elkan, now lie back down and close your eyes. I'll put a dressing on your heel."

Elkan lies back down and closes his eyes. He feels a hand lift his heel as something warm is placed on it. The warmth travels up his leg through his body and into his head. There is such a relaxing feeling that Elkan's mind starts wandering and thinking about home, his family, his friends, his dog, and everything that he has done to hurt people. He starts remembering all of the lies he's told and starts to thrash around and weep.

Suddenly, Elkan is jarred awake by Kamali shaking him.

"Elkan! Elkan! Wake up! You're dreaming! Wake up!"

"Wha? Huh … What's going on?"

"I woke up with your foot in my side and then you suddenly started kicking and you kicked me in my stomach. Were you dreaming?"

"No … Yeah … Uh … I don't know! I thought I was awake but maybe I was dreaming I was awake. But then I would have been dreaming that I was dreaming I was awake … or something like that!"

"Are you okay?"

"Other than my heel I'm fine."

"What about your heel?"

"You know, the cut. The one you put something on to help it heal."

"I was sleeping, Elkan. I never placed anything on your heel."

"Sure your did! See!"

Elkan lifts his leg to show Kamali his foot.

"I don't see anything Elkan."

Elkan bends his knee to look at his heel himself but doesn't see anything. No cut. No dressing.

Completely embarrassed and confused he says, "I guess I was dreaming the whole thing. That's really weird."

"You're under a lot of stress Elkan. You have learned a lot of new truths lately that contradict your previous understanding. It's okay to process it all, but try not to let it overwhelm you. The images in your mind are not truth. There is no need to worry. I am here with you."

"Yeah, maybe you're right. The sun is starting to rise so let's just get up and get going to the tower."

"Let's!"

Elkan and Kamali splash their faces with the water from the clay washbasin, gather themselves together, and walk out the door and down the steps. Kamali knocks on the front door of the house as he did the previous night. When the man comes to the door, Kamali thanks him for his hospitality and they depart.

Retracing their steps from last night, they arrive at the main road again. Kamali asks a goat shepherd how to get to the tower. The shepherd steps to the side of the road and draws some lines in the dirt with his staff. As he explains the lines, he also points further up the road, correlating the direction of his pointing with that of each line in the sand. Kamali thanks him, and he and Elkan start in the direction the shepherd pointed first.

"He said it is a morning's journey from here."

Elkan looks to the East at the tower reaching high above everything else and replies, "How are we ever going to find the key in this huge city? There's gotta be a million people here with miles of area to cover."

"How would you ever find a key on a stone beach or in a dense forest? Why question now?"

"I don't know. It just looks so impossible–but you're right again. We'll find it no matter what! I won't quit until we do. I want to see what's in that chest that's so important."

"That's the spirit, Elkan."

They head North on the road that will eventually take them East to the tower. Along the way Elkan takes in his surroundings; the blue sky with puffy white clouds that remind him of the time he smeared his dad's shaving cream all over the bathroom mirror. He sees the green trees and plants with their fruit and flowers. The people along the way are dirty and dusty from the sand, and the houses are made of mud and sticks. He observes people all around—living their lives and going about their daily duties without missing a beat.

A couple hours later, the narrow street they are traveling ends in a large open area with workers baking bricks of clay mixed with straw. Some men are hurrying about directing workers, yet others are transporting materials. Everyone is moving like ants scurrying about, gathering building materials for their hill—what looks like chaos on the surface is really a carefully organized dance. A little give here and a little take there. One misstep and someone could end up seriously injured, if not dead. A camel approaches Elkan, looks at him, and spits on him.

"Eww, how nasty!" Elkan shouts with disgust as he wipes his face with his sleeve.

After the camel leaves and Elkan gets over the embarrassment, he leans his head back as his eyes follow the tower from ground to sky. He stares in utter amazement at the size of the structure.

"Quite the project isn't it?" a voice says from behind them.

Elkan and Kamali turn to see a middle-aged man with a beard and much nicer robe than most.

"I have been watching them for years as they focus every ounce of energy on this tower for Nimrod, the mighty hunter. He has been elevated to the status of a god, while the one true God is forgotten.

"Shalom! My name is Eber, son of Selah son of Arphaxad."

Elkan's heart jumps to his throat. "Arphaxad, the son of Shem son of Noah?"

"That would be the one. How do you know him?"

Kamali jumps in, "He is a student of history."

"But we were …" Elkan begins to say when Kamali places his hand in front of Elkan's face to silence him.

"As I was saying, he is a student of history and we are here to see the great tower that Nimrod is building."

"Yes, the great tower that everyone wants to see. The tower of arrogance and disobedience! The tower that will send a curse down on us all."

"What do you mean?" Elkan asks.

"Our Lord has told us from the early days to fill the earth, but everyone has gathered in a few cities here in the land of Shinar - Erech, Accad, Calneh, Assyria, Nineveh, Rehoboth Ir, Calah, Resen between Nineveh and Calah, that *is* the principal city, and here in Bab-ilu where they build this tower."

"Why are they building it?" asks Elkan.

"They say to make a name for themselves so that they won't be scattered abroad over the face of the earth. I say it's an altar to Nimrod. He has made a great name for himself as a great hunter before the Lord and wants to elevate himself to that of a god, which is why he has to build a man made structure to reach the heavens. It's blasphemy!"

"Didn't they learn from the days of Noah?" asks Elkan.

"The history has not been passed down accurately through the generations and many are choosing to ignore the past.

They think the rainbow covenant gives them free will to do what they please because there is no fear of absolute destruction again."

"How can they be so blind?" Elkan questions.

Kamali reminds Elkan, "Remember, we all have free will, just as Adam had free will to choose to eat the forbidden fruit. We all know the difference between right and wrong, it's our choice which path to take. Unfortunately, many choose the path away from God and toward destruction. Always ask what His will is for you when making decisions."

"Very well said. You have a wise teacher young man."

"By the way, my name is Kamali and this lad is Elkan."

"Shalom!" replies Eber as they embrace each other in a hug. "Will you join me for dinner with my son?"

"Of course we will! We would be honored." replies Kamali.

"Good. Then we better go find him. He's at the market with some of our sheep."

When they get to the market a young boy, younger than Elkan, comes running up to Eber with excitement.

"We sold all of them Father! See, here's the money!"

Eber holds out his hand and the young boy places a bag in his hand as it jingles with coins.

"This is my son Peleg. I have another son, Joktan, at home tending the flock. We come here monthly to sell some ewes and to buy other necessities."

Peleg clasps his hands and bows his head to Kamali and Elkan. "Shalom," he says.

Elkan and Kamali do the same–"Shalom."

Within minutes the sky turns very dark and people start rushing around. The wind picks up and starts blowing vendors' tents over. Chickens trying to fly their way to safety get picked up by the gusts and blown through the streets. Everyone is heading to shelter as quickly as they can. Dust is getting in their eyes and their tunics are flapping on their legs like the sails on the ship. The sand is beating away at any exposed skin, and it quickly becomes painful.

"Follow me!" exclaims Eber. "I have a key to my cousin's house not far from here. We'll find safety there."

In an instant, a blinding light appears in the sky over the tower. Everyone looks to the ground and tries covering their eyes. A deafening clap of thunder is heard and it vibrates in their chests. Screams are heard everywhere. The top portion of the tower explodes, and bricks rain down over the entire city. Pieces of brick and wood are falling around Elkan, Kamali, Eber and Peleg. A thundering rumble shakes the entire city. Buildings collapse. People continue screaming and running throughout the streets looking for shelter. Elkan is terrified and wonders how much longer it will last.

Then, as quickly as it started, it's over. The sky opens up and the sun comes out again. Many people lie scattered about injured or sobbing with their heads in their hands. There are men crying out, tearing their robes.

"Are you okay?" asks Eber.

"Yes, I'm fine," replies Kamali.

"I'm okay," exclaims Elkan.

"Is it over Father?" Peleg asks with a worried voice.

"It's over son."

"Good," Peleg sighs as he embraces Eber.

As they continue to Eber's cousin's house, they pass many more injured and dead. There are women holding loved ones who have been injured. Children are crying, standing, and turning in circles looking for their parents. Men are digging through the debris searching for family. When they arrive at the house, they find a pile of rubble. Immediately Eber rushes to the rubble. Seeing signs of death within the debris, Eber cries out and tears his robe dropping the key in his hand. He falls to his knees sobbing. As he turns his head toward Elkan and Kamali, he stares past them. Quickly rising to his feet, he runs past them with his arms outstretched.

Elkan and Kamali turn to see what's happening. Another man is running toward Eber with his arms outstretched. "Cousin!" Eber exclaims as they meet each other and embrace tightly, both of them sobbing. Eber says something to the other man and the man looks at him strangely saying something in return.

They both quickly move apart and start trying to talk over each other, getting louder and louder. They both have panic on their faces. Elkan understands what Eber is saying as he gets louder, but can't understand a word the other man is saying.

Elkan looks around and sees similar situations all around. People are having trouble understanding each other. Elkan walks over to where Eber had fallen to his knees and picks up the key. It looks very similar to the last key, but with a triangular finial as opposed to a loop.

Eber returns to the group. "We must go!" He continues walking without even looking at his cousin's house. The group follows in silence as they walk through the city and to the main road heading out of the city. Along the way there is nothing but destruction and confusion - People yelling and crying at each other in different languages.

At the edge of the city, Eber turns to Kamali and Elkan. "I told him not to go in that way. I told him not to forget the God of our people, but he chose to worship Nimrod and that blasted tower of his. 'Gether,' I said, 'don't forsake your heritage,' but he didn't listen—no one listened. Now look, God has confused our language, and I can't even communicate with parts of my family. It is time that Peleg and I return home to mourn. Shalom my friends." He and Peleg turn and head into the wilderness.

"Shalom!" Elkan and Kamali reply, and they start trying to find someone who can understand them to get directions back to the river. Suddenly Elkan turns, holds up the key and yells, "Eber! Your key! You forgot the key to your cousin's house."

"I don't need it anymore!" he yells back. "I have no cousin and he has no house!" and Eber turns away and continues walking.

Eventually they find a woman who understands them and gives direction to the river. They discover that it is just a short distance away. Kamali and Elkan quickly rush to the river and find that it is further up stream than where they arrived. Fortunately there is a boatman that understands them and offers to take them down river to their dinghy. Once they arrive at their dinghy, they quickly untie it and start toward the mouth of the river.

By this time the sun is setting and darkness is falling. As they row down river, Elkan looks to the East at the tower and barely sees anything but the silhouette of dust and smoke rising into the air.

"Can you explain to me what exactly just happened?" Elkan asks Kamali.

"Just as Eber said. God told Noah to go forth and spread across the earth. Not everyone through the generations listened and they started elevating themselves, especially Nimrod, to god status. So God destroyed the tower and confused the language. Until today, there was one world language, now there are many with many more to come over the next several generations."

"So now what happens to the people?"

"They will search out those who speak the same language and congregate together. Then they will have to disperse across the earth to establish their own villages and cities. Unfortunately for them, they are faced with a sudden loss of information from knowledgeable and skilled people as they can no longer exchange ideas and work together as one large group. They will have to take the knowledge and skills of those who speak their language and start over from there. This will lead to some advanced groups and some more primitive groups."

By this time they arrive at *The Spirit of God* and climb aboard. They head to Kamali's quarters continuing their conversation. Elkan is so tired and distraught over the events of the day that he doesn't even try the key in the lock. Kamali pulls the map from the safe and, just as he always does, rolls it out across the table.

"How can God do something like that?" Elkan asks.

"He is a just God and judges the obedience of man. You should know that from the garden, as well as from Noah."

"I guess it's just hard to understand. He can't expect people to be perfect and be like Him."

"Remember Elkan, in the beginning everything was perfect and then Adam sinned. From that original sin man has had a rebellious heart, thus man's constant disobedience. God has given man laws to live by. But they don't heed, therefore God judges them for their disobedience. For the wages of sin is death."

"I guess," Elkan replies sadly as he turns to look at the map.

This time when Elkan sees the map, he sees many different names all over the map. Some he recognizes like Babylon, Arphaxad, Nimrod, Lot, Egypt, Cush, Tarsus, and many others.

"Notice the name—Sea of Confusion," Kamali questions. "And the cities across the map, many named after people? The confusion of languages has a profound effect on the people of the world forever. Many nations will grow up out of this spreading, including Germany, Italy, China, Mexico, Australia, America, and so on. This spreading across the earth will also account for skin color. Most people now have medium brown skin. Those who move to hotter areas of the earth, like Africa, will develop darker skin and those who migrate to cooler parts of the earth, like England, will develop lighter skin as a general rule. Do you understand?"

"So that is why each country has its own language and we have the different races?"

"Yes and no. That is why there are languages for each country, but remember, there is only one race, the human race—just with different skin tones."

"I never thought of it that way. That's great! So now I can say that everyone is truly created equal, and I'm related to everyone. The earth is one great big family."

"Yes, you can say that!"

"Cool! Now, can I try the key?"

"Go for it!"

Elkan runs to the chest and pulls all of the keys out of his bag, carefully placing each one into its respective lock until he gets to the new one. With great care he inserts the newest key into the fourth lock and turns. With ease it drops open. "We're half way there!"

"Only three more to go," replies Kamali. "Only three more."

Elkan locks each one back up and removes the keys placing each one carefully back into his ditty bag.

"I'm going to get some sleep now," Elkan suggests. "I'm really tired."

"Good night, Elkan."

As he leaves Kamali's room, he glances at the map to see where they are headed next. He can't see anything that would give him a clue, so he heads off to bed.

CHAPTER 5

A GATHERING

After Elkan awakes he starts his usual routine of heading above deck and looking for Kamali. Knowing exactly where to look, he heads toward the bow of the ship. But he doesn't see Kamali there this morning. Panicking, he runs back below deck and rushes to Kamali's room.

He pounds on the door. "Kamali! Captain Kamali! Are you in there?"

"No, I'm right here," Kamali replies from behind. "What's the problem boy?"

"I went up to the deck and you weren't at your usual place at the bow."

"No, I wasn't was I? I was checking on our supplies, and it seems as though we are getting low on food. We will have to restock at the next town."

"What town is that?"

"It's known as the 'House of Bread!'" he states arriving on deck as he points to a land that is lush with rolling hills and olive trees.

"A city known as the 'House of Bread?' I guess that would be a good place to get food. Can I order a sandwich like at a deli?" Elkan laughs sarcastically. "But there's nothing there but hills and fields."

"Don't jest at what you don't understand. Secondly, beyond what the eye can see is the city, and that is where we are going."

"Yes, Sir! Captain Salami, Sir!" Elkan firmly states while saluting Kamali.

"If you wish to successfully complete this journey, you will have respect for me and you will not have a flippant attitude!" Kamali commands harshly.

"Yes, Sir. Sorry, Kamali. I just think it's a funny name for a city," Elkan sheepishly replies.

Kamali softens his voice. "I understand that, Elkan. But you should never show disrespect to others."

"What you currently see is the hill country of Judah. The high hills over there are where we will be going. This area is known as Beit-Sahour, and the town known as the 'House of Bread' is called Beit-Lahm."

The ship comes to rest and Elkan and Kamali once again shove off in the dinghy.

Once on land the boat is secured and they start in the direction of the city. Walking through the fields, a short while later, they end up on a main road. The road is very busy with people, most of them heading in one direction, the direction Elkan and Kamali are heading. Out in the fields they see shepherds tending to their flocks.

"This must be a very busy city," Elkan comments.

"Not generally this busy," Kamali responds with a question in his voice. "Sir," Kamali asks a man leading a donkey upon which rides a young expectant mother, "why is the road so crowded?"

"Have you not heard? Caesar Augustus has declared a census to register the whole world, so everyone is on their way to their ancestral town to do so."

No sooner does the man finish his sentence than Elkan stops dead in his tracks. Kamali quickly thanks the man and turns to Elkan. Then he turns his head in the direction of where Elkan is looking. Standing off to the side of the road are three Roman soldiers. Dressed to the hilt, they are wearing their helmets that have the red fluffy mohawk, the plate armor on their shoulders and chest, tunics, sandals, spear, and sword. They are very well built. They are talking amongst themselves but keeping a close eye on what's happening around them.

"Come on Elkan, you'll see plenty of those from here on out," Kamali exclaims.

"Those are real ... Roman ... soldiers!" Elkan exclaims.

"Yes they are, now don't look amazed. They'll see you as being suspicious and we don't need to deal with the Roman government. Now let's get moving."

They continue on their journey to the city. By the time they reach the city, the streets are so crowded it's like a mall parking lot at Christmas. They can hardly move without bumping into someone. There seems to be Roman soldiers on nearly every corner. They stop at several inns but can't find one that has any vacancy. They spend several hours moving throughout the city looking for a place to stay when finally they find someone willing to share their room for a portion of the cost.

As the night sky appears, the city is still bustling with people—people who can't find a place to stay for the night. The room they are staying in is again on the second floor and as Elkan looks down, he sees the man and woman that they had spoken with earlier taking their donkey to the stable behind and beneath the house across the street.

Off in the distance, in the region known as Beit-Sahour,

where shepherds are tending their flock, a very bright light appears. So bright it looks like a star resting on the horizon. It lasts for only a minute or two when suddenly it gets even brighter, only this time it is in the sky. Now it is so bright that it looks like a city all lit up and drowning out the moon, but not really affecting the light in their current city of Beit-Lahm. Then, just as quickly as it appeared, the night sky over the fields becomes dark again.

Elkan turns and notices Kamali behind him. He was there the entire time and saw it all himself.

"What do you suppose that light was?" Elkan asks.

"I guess we'll find out in the morning. For now, let's get some rest."

They and their roommates get situated and talk for a little while before calling it a night and falling asleep.

The next morning they awake to the loud noise of the crowds in the street. They head down to the street to start looking for a market or someplace to stock up on some food. When they arrive on the street there are some shepherds, without their sheep, talking to everyone that passes.

One of them comes up to Elkan and Kamali and says, "Listen to what I have to say. An angel of the Lord stood before us last night while we were tending our sheep. And the glory of the Lord shined around him. And the angel said to us, 'I bring you good news of great joy which will be to all people. For today there is born in the city of David a Savior, who is Christ the Lord.'" He continues enthusiastically, "And then the angel of the Lord told us, 'this will be a sign to you: You will find a Babe wrapped in swaddling cloths, lying in a manger.' And then suddenly with the angel there was a congregation of the heavenly host praising God and saying:

'Glory to God in the highest, and on earth peace, goodwill toward men!'

So we decided to come to Beit-Lahm to see for ourselves this thing that has come to pass, which the Lord has made known to us."

By this time a crowd had started to gather. Everyone who heard it marveled at these things.

The shepherd continues, "We came as quickly as we could and we found a woman and man with the Babe lying in a manger."

And when the shepherds were through, they returned to the fields, glorifying and praising God for all the things that they had heard and seen, as it was told them.

"These are truly special times, Elkan," Kamali says with a smile. "Truly special times."

Now, because of the crowd the shepherds drew there were a number of Roman soldiers nearby. After the shepherds left, so did the crowds, as did the soldiers. Kamali and Elkan begin their search for food to take back to the ship. Everywhere they search there is little food to be found—not nearly enough to sustain them for a journey on the ship. As the mid-day sun starts setting, Kamali suggests they look a little further north in a city called Jerusalem. "It is a larger city and has a temple built for King Herod, so food should be more plentiful and it is only a few miles away."

They find the main road, the ancient caravan route, and travel throughout the crowds going to and from Jerusalem. What would normally take about an hour takes them much longer because of the huge crowd of people traveling, but they finally arrive at the outer walls of the city. It is a great stone wall surrounding the city and reaching what looks like twenty feet high. They enter through what is called the Essene Gate into the lower part of the city. Again, the streets are crowded with people and soldiers are all around.

Just as in Biet-Lahm, they search around for someplace to

stay for the night and someplace that might have enough food for them to take back to the ship. Fortunately they do find a place to stay, but have little luck finding someone willing to sell them enough food to meet their needs. Elkan and Kamali end up staying in Jerusalem for a few weeks until the crowds disperse and vendors are able to stock up on food and sell larger quantities. During that time, they explore the city and get to know it fairly well. Elkan likes to visit the Temple with all of its grandeur. It is under construction and has been for many, many years. It towers over the city and has many rooms. From one side Elkan can see the beautiful valley full of lush grass and plants where often times sheep will graze on the hillside. The temple is adorned in gold and precious stones. It is said to be one of Herod's great masterpieces.

Often he sees a nice, gentle old man hanging around minding his own business and not bothering anyone. Then one day, after about a month or so, Elkan and Kamali see him approach a young couple with a newborn baby.

"Isn't that the man and woman we saw on the way to Biet-Lahm? The one's who were taking their donkey into the stable behind the house across the street from where we stayed?" Elkan asks Kamali.

"It does appear so, doesn't it?" Kamali replies.

The old man approaches the couple and says something Elkan can't hear. Elkan and Kamali move a little closer to see the infant. He has a perfect little face with puckered lips and bright eyes. He is alert and looking around at everything. They can see a small lock of hair peaking through His wraps. And He's the quietest baby Elkan has ever seen. The old man takes the baby into his arms and says something. Then the man hands the baby back to His mother and says something else, smiles, and leaves the temple glowing like a young child himself.

Elkan chases after the old man to find out exactly what he said to the couple. He leaves that part of the temple and looks around seeing no sign of him. Another man passes by and Elkan asks if he saw an old man leaving this part of the temple.

"You mean Simeon?" the stranger replies. "No, I haven't seen him today." With that he continues on into the temple.

Elkan turns to go back to Kamali. When he gets back to him, the couple with the baby is gone.

Disappointed, Elkan comments to Kamali that there is something about that couple. "Why do we keep running into them?"

"I can't tell you," Kamali replies. "Now let's go try to find some food and get going back to the ship."

Elkan and Kamali leave the temple and find a merchant who has enough food and is willing to sell it. Then they start back toward Biet-Lahm, as they must pass back through to get to *The Spirit of God*. Along the way Elkan is trying to piece together the strange things that have happened on this leg of the journey. First there was the crowded city because of the census, then there was the strange bright light in the fields of Biet-Sahour, and the shepherds rambling on about an angel of the Lord and a savior being born, and all along this couple keeps showing up until the old man, Simeon, takes their baby and rambles on to himself about the Lord's salvation and parting in peace and the fall and rising of Israel. It almost sounds like the Christmas story he thinks to himself.

Suddenly Elkan turns to Kamali and shouts, "Bethlehem! Beit-Lahm is Bethlehem! It makes sense now!"

Kamali looks at Elkan in wonder, "Okay … ?"

"The couple is Mary and Joseph. They were going to Bethlehem for the census. Mary was expecting a child, but not Joseph's child, God's child! And the bright light in the fields must have been the angel the shepherds were talking about and the baby Jesus must have been born across the street that night. And that would explain why the old man said what he said about the baby. We saw Jesus, Kamali! We saw the baby Jesus!" Elkan continues with excitement. "And I didn't get to say 'Hi' to Him. I was too stupid to see what was right in front of my eyes when I went chasing off after something else," he suddenly realizes with sadness.

"Do not be sad, Elkan," Kamali responds. "For you have heard that unto us a child is born, unto us a son is given and his name shall be called Wonderful, Counselor, The mighty God, The everlasting Father, The Prince of Peace."

"Will we see Him again?" Elkan asks.

"See Jesus? You can count on it!" Kamali replies.

They enter Bethlehem and Elkan wants to go back to the house Mary and Joseph stayed at to see the manger where Jesus lie. When they arrive, they find a cave-like basement behind the house where animals are kept. And there in the corner of the stable is a manger.

"It's nothing like we see on all the Christmas cards and in books," Elkan comments. "It's much less fantastic than those pictures. It's so ... so much simpler."

Elkan goes up to the manger and kneels down next to it. He looks around and then back at the manger, brushing his hands over some of the straw, imagining what occurred that night right across the street from where he was sleeping. Then he rises up and says, "Let's get back to the ship," and starts heading back to the street.

Along the way, Elkan finds himself humming the song *Away in a Manger*. Once on the main road they took into the city, one of the shepherds that was telling everyone about the events of that special night when Jesus was born is herding his sheep across the way. He looks up and sees Kamali and Elkan.

He walks over to Elkan and says, "I have been instructed to give you this," as he reaches into his own ditty bag and pulls out a key. The key is brass with a six-pointed star on it. "The key to the 'House of Bread.' May you always be full of the bread of life–the star of David, to remember your inheritance." And with that, he turns and continues herding his sheep across the road into a new field for them to graze.

Elkan shouts out to the shepherd, "Thank you! How did you know?"

Without turning around he points his staff toward the sky and shouts, "He knows!" and continues on his way.

In sheer excitement, Elkan takes off running and jumping, urging Kamali to pick up the pace. Eventually they arrive at the dinghy, load it up, and head back to the ship.

When they arrive at the ship, Elkan helps Kamali take the food to the galley and then rushes to Kamali's quarters to try the key.

Elkan is standing at the door holding his ditty bag in his hand when Kamali arrives to open the door. As he does, Elkan rushes in and quickly, with clockwork precision, inserts the first four keys and opens the locks. Now for the fifth key, the one that tells him this leg of the journey is complete. Elkan lifts the lock and begins to place the key in it when he can't find the keyhole. In frustration and fear he starts to whimper.

"Where's the keyhole? How can the lock not have a keyhole?"

"The city of David, Elkan. Remember, Jesus was born in the city of David."

"What's that have to do with the lock?"

"The *Star* of Bethlehem … "

"What? What do you mean the city of David and S*tar* of Bethlehem?

The room is silent for a moment as Elkan pauses to think.

"Why do you always have to speak in riddles?"

"I speak in truth not riddles. I just don't always tell you everything. Some things you have to figure out for yourself or you won't learn the truth."

After a few more moments of staring at the lock and then at the key, his vision narrows on the key overlapping the lock and realizes that the back of the key, the part with the star is the exact same star and same size as the one on the lock.

"David's Star!" Elkan shouts. "It's the Star of David that is the key, not the shaft of the key!" He places the back of the key into the star on the lock and it fits perfectly. He gives it a turn and the lock drops open.

"See, Elkan, sometimes you have to look at things differently. I've been telling you not to always assume what you think you know but to look for the real truth."

"Woo Hoo! Five down and two to go! Hurry, go get the map out and let me see it."

As Elkan re-locks the locks and places the keys back into his bag, Kamali retrieves the map from the safe and rolls it out over the table.

Elkan's eyes quickly scan the map for anything new that has appeared, and behold, he sees that the name of the sea is the Sea of Christ, and he sees Bethlehem, Jerusalem, a shepherd's staff, and a lamb outside of Bethlehem with a star above. He also sees a group of men with gifts in their hands.

"Are those the wise men?" Elkan asks. "I don't remember seeing them."

"They were there, Elkan, just not when we were. They came to visit when we were up in Jerusalem. And see there?" Kamali points to an image of two adults and a very young child and donkey on a path headed toward a land called Egypt.

"That is the Holy Family fleeing to Egypt," Kamali continues.

"Why were they fleeing?"

"Remember the king who wanted the Magi to let him know where the newborn king was so that he could worship Him?"

"Yeah, King Herod. What about him?" No sooner does Elkan speak those words than he remembers what he learned in Sunday school. "The wise men were supposed to tell the king where baby Jesus was and they didn't, so Herod ordered all children under the age of two to be killed. That's when Mary and Joseph fled to Egypt, to save baby Jesus. I get it now! I never realized that all of that was true. I always thought this stuff was just stories—but it's not, is it?"

"You're learning, Elkan. You're finally starting to understand the truth."

"So what's the next place we go to?" Elkan looks at the map but has no clue where they will be heading next. "Can we head there tonight?"

"Are you in a hurry?" Kamali laughs.

"We only have two more to go and I want to see what this treasure is and who it goes to!"

"Well then, we mustn't waste any time must we?"

They head above deck. Once up there, Elkan realizes that they've already set sail.

"When did we set sail?" he asks Kamali confused.

"While you were trying the key of course." Kamali smiles that smile of knowing something that no one else does.

Sitting at the bow of the ship, Elkan looks out over the moonlit ocean and reflects on the journey to this point. *We've been on the Sea of Creation where God created everything in the universe including the universe itself, the Sea of Corruption where Adam and Eve sinned and were kicked out of the Garden of Eden,* the Sea of Catastrophe with Noah's ark and the worldwide flood, the Sea of Confusion where God confused the languages at the Tower of Babel and now the Sea of Christ with Jesus' birth, he thinks to himself. *What could possibly be next?*

Elkan quickly jumps up and runs over to Kamali. "Tell me we aren't going to Easter!"

"What?" Kamali questions.

"Please tell me we're not going to Easter. I don't want to see Jesus' crucifixion!"

"Why don't you want to see Jesus crucified?"

"Why would I?" Elkan responds angrily. "Why would I want to see anyone get killed?"

"Ahh! I see. You still have a lot to learn and two legs of the journey left. Let's get some rest and ease your worries."

Kamali places his arm around Elkan and starts walking him to his room. The entire way Elkan continues questioning where they are headed next and asking Kamali to promise they won't see Jesus killed and Kamali always replies, "We'll go where *The Spirit* leads and only the truth will be revealed to you. Besides, why worry about tomorrow–it will take care of itself."

They arrive at Elkan's room and Kamali opens the door, nudges Elkan in and says, "Good night."

Unable to get to sleep right away, Elkan tosses and turns swinging back and forth in his hammock. After what seems like forever, he finally falls asleep.

CHAPTER 6

THE CONQUERING KING

When Elkan awakes, he again follows his routine of heading to the bow of the ship to meet Kamali for the morning. They are already anchored, and Elkan sees land immediately upon arriving above deck.

"That was quick. We must not have gone very far," Elkan comments.

"*The Spirit of God* can move swiftly or it can move slowly. That we do not control."

They quickly prepare the dinghy and head ashore. They travel over the desert land until they find a road. The only things they see are olive trees, fig trees, and a few other sparse plants and grass. They travel for hours upon this road before they see their first sign of life. Another shepherd is herding his flock of sheep a little in the distance where there is more grass. They can hear the baa's of the sheep and the shepherd's voice talking to them, but Elkan can't understand what he is saying. Eventually they see, off in the distance, a hill with a crowd of people gathering.

"What's going on there?" Elkan asks.

"Let's go find out," Kamali replies.

So they head in that direction and some time later come upon numerous additional people heading that way. As they arrive at the hillside, hundreds of people stand quietly listening to a man teaching. Elkan and Kamali fight the crowd and work their way closer to the man to hear more clearly what he is saying. And when they are finally in a place they can hear him clearly they hear:

And when you pray, you should not be like the hypocrites, for they love to pray standing in the synagogues and in the corners of the streets, that they may be seen by men. Truly I tell you, they have their reward. But you, when you pray, go into your closet, and shut your door, then pray to your Father, which is in secret; and your Father, who sees in secret will reward you openly. But when you pray, do not use worthless repetitions, like the wicked they think that they will be heard for their numerous words. Therefore, do not be like them for your Father knows what things you need before you ask Him. When you pray, say, 'Our Father who is in heaven, Holy is your name. Your kingdom come, Your will be done on earth, as it is in heaven. Give us this day our daily bread. And forgive us our sins, as we forgive those who sin against us. And keep us from temptation, and deliver us from evil for yours is the kingdom, and the power, and the glory, forever. Amen.' For if you forgive men their sins, your heavenly Father will also forgive you. But if you do not forgive men their sins, neither will your Father forgive yours.

"Is that who I think it is?" Elkan excitedly whispers to Kamali. "Is that really Jesus? He just said the Lord's Prayer."

"Shhh! Yes it is and yes He did, now listen!" Kamali whispers back sternly.

As they refocus on Jesus he continues,

Do not hoard your treasures here on earth, where moths and rust destroy, and where thieves break in and steal but gather up your treasures in heaven, where moths and rust do not destroy, and where thieves do not break in or steal. For where your treasure is, your heart will be there also. The eye is the light of the body, so if your eye is good, your whole body will be full of light. But if your eye is evil, your whole body will be full of darkness. Therefore, if the light that is in you is darkness, how great is that darkness! No man can serve two masters for either he will hate one, and love the other or else he will cling to the one, and despise the other. You cannot serve God and earthly things. Therefore I tell you, do not worry about your life, what you will eat, or what you will drink; nor for your body, what you will wear. Is life not more than food, and the body more than clothes? Observe the birds of the air: for they do not sow seeds, neither do they reap the harvest, nor gather into barns; yet your heavenly Father feeds them. Are you not much better than they are? Which of you by worrying can add one cubit to his size? And why concern yourself about clothes? Behold the lilies of the field, how they grow; they do not work, neither do they make clothes. Yet I say to you, even Solomon in all his glory was not dressed as well as one of these. In as much as God clothes the grass of the field, which is in the field today, and tomorrow is thrown into the oven, will he not clothe you even more, Oh you of little faith? So, do not worry, saying, 'What will we eat?' or, 'What will we drink?' or, 'How will we get our clothes?' The Gentiles seek after all these things, but your heavenly Father knows what your needs are. Therefore, seek first the kingdom of God, and His righteousness; and all these things will be taken care of for you. Consequently do not worry about tomorrow because tomorrow will take care of itself. There is enough concern for today; you do not need to add to it by worrying about tomorrow.

Do not judge so that you will not be judged. For with what judgment you judge, you shall be judged: and with what measurement you use, it will be used to measure you. And why do you focus on the speck that is in your brother's eye, but ignore the log that is in your own eye? Or how will you say to your brother, "Let me remove the speck from your eye" and, behold, a log is in your own eye? You hypocrite! First cast out the log that is in your own eye; and then you will be able to see clearly to remove the speck from your brother's eye.

"I've heard all of this before!" Elkan whispers excitedly to Kamali.

"Of course you have, boy! Now listen more and learn!" Kamali replies.

Elkan quickly turns to face Jesus again and listens.

... Ask, and it will be given to you; seek, and you will find; knock, and it will be opened for you. For every one that asks receives; and he that seeks finds; and to him that knocks it shall be opened. What man is there among you, whom if his son asks for bread, will give him a stone? Or if he asks for a fish, will give him a snake? If you then, being evil, know how to give good gifts to your children, how much more will your heavenly Father give good things to those who ask Him?

"Why would someone's father give them a stone or snake to eat?" Elkan wonders aloud.

"That's the point, now stick a sock in it and listen!" replies Kamali.

... Therefore treat people the same way you want them to treat you, for this is the law and what is expected of you. Enter in at the thin gate: for the gate is wide and the way is broad, that leads to death, and many will enter through it. Because thin is the gate, and narrow is the way, that leads to life, and few will find it ...

"Just like the one key, huh, Kamali?" Elkan chimes in.

"Yes, Elkan! Now listen," Kamali chides.

... Beware of false prophets, who approach you in sheep's clothing, but inwardly they are ravening wolves. You will know them by their fruits. Do men gather grapes of thorns, or figs of thistles? Even so every good tree produces good fruit; but a corrupt tree yields evil fruit. A good tree cannot beget evil fruit; neither can a corrupt tree bring forth good fruit. Every tree that does not produce good fruit is cut down, and burned. Therefore, you will know them by their fruits.

Not every one that says to Me, "Lord, Lord," will enter into the kingdom of heaven, but only those

JOHN *and* KATHY EYTCHISON

who do My Father's will which is in heaven. Many will say to Me in that day, "Lord, Lord, have we not prophesied in your name? And in your name cast out demons? And in your name have we done many wonderful things?" Then will I say to them, "I never knew you; leave me, you who acted in My name but for selfish reasons." Therefore, whosoever hears what I say, and does them, I will compare him to a wise man, who built his house upon a rock. And the rain fell, the floods came, and the winds blew beating upon that house; and it did not fall because it was built upon a rock. And every one that hears what I say, and does not do them, will be like a foolish man, who built his house on the sand. The rain fell, the floods came, the winds blew, beating against that house; and it fell, and great was its fall.

And with that Jesus is finished teaching and heads down the mountain followed by the crowd of people, everyone bumping into each other as He passes by Elkan and Kamali. A few steps later He stops and turns, looking at Elkan, and then turns back to continue down the mountain.

Elkan and Kamali follow and manage to stay close to Jesus and His disciples. Along the way Elkan tells Kamali, "At one time or another I have heard everything that Jesus said. It's amazing how all of it is true. They really are the words of Jesus."

"Of course they are really the words of Jesus. He said them," Kamali responds with a snicker.

"Well, yeah, I know that, but I thought He didn't ... well He did, but ... I mean, I know He really said them, but I didn't know that He ... *really* ... said ... them. Oh, you know what I mean!" Elkan says frustrated.

"What you're saying is that you knew He really said those things but you didn't believe it."

"Well ... yeah, I guess. But I did ... I mean do believe it."

"You mean you do believe it *now*."

When they reach the bottom of the mountain a man with really bad sores and flies all over his body comes up to Jesus worshiping Him and saying, "Lord, if you will, can you heal me?" Many of the people that are standing near the man step away from him. Jesus reaches his hand out and replies, "I will. Be healed." Immediately the man's sores are healed, even the nasty open ones.

Then Jesus says to him, "See that you tell no one' but go, show yourself to the priest and present the offering that Moses commanded, as a testimony to them."

So the man runs off to do as Jesus told him.

Elkan looks at Kamali and asks, "What was wrong with that man?"

And Kamali replies, "He has ... or had, leprosy, a very terrible disease."

From there, Kamali pulls Elkan aside and tells him they must find a place to stay, and they head to a city called Capernaum along the Sea of Galilee.

"But I want to stay with Jesus!" Elkan fusses.

"I promise we will see Him again, now let's go."

So they leave Jesus, His disciples, and the crowd and go to find lodging in Capernaum. When they arrive, they find a place to stay close to the beach.

A couple hours later they are settled in and Elkan is looking out the window at the sea. He is watching the fishing boats coming and going. He hears the loud noise of a crowd and then sees Jesus and the disciples, being followed by hundreds or thousands. This time Jesus and the disciples get on a fishing-boat and head out to sea. The crowds that were following Him slowly settle down. Elkan can hear babies crying and children laughing as they play. There are few birds in the sky and the waves crash against the shore. Clouds are rolling in from sea.

A wind blows. They look out over the sea and notice a dark sky with a great storm building up. Very quickly the waves get bigger and bigger until, within minutes, Elkan can't even see the boat Jesus is on. Some of the crowd gets restless as they are witnessing the same thing and are concerned for Jesus and the disciples. Elkan can hear gasps throughout the crowd and babies start crying more. Then, moments later, the sea calms and the winds stop. The clouds open up to show the light of the moon.

"That was a strange storm with its sudden rise and then calming," Elkan comments to Kamali.

"Oh, you of little faith. When will you understand?"

"Understand what?"

"Truth! And the power of truth! You know that Jesus is not just any ordinary man. You've been taught it. You've seen Him and heard Him, but you don't seem to know Him."

"How can I know Him when I haven't met Him?"

"He is truth. You know His Creation. You know Him in your head. You need to know Him in your heart - and you soon will."

And with that they lie down to sleep.

When they awake the next morning it is already near noontime. The noise of a crowd and people talking is what wakes them. Elkan looks out the window and sees people hustling about and talking with excitement.

"What's going on?" Elkan turns to ask Kamali.

"What was going on yesterday? Do you think that the same won't occur today?"

"Everyone is heading to listen to Jesus?"

"What do you think?"

"Then let's follow them and hear Him again today!" Elkan spouts out as if he was just given the greatest gift he could imagine. He can't get enough of Jesus' teachings.

They prepare themselves and leave to join the crowd. They follow the crowd out of the city and along the sea. Along the way they hear people talking.

"Did you hear about Jesus commanding the demons into a pig?" says one man to another.

"I heard that He healed a royal official's son without even being there. He simply spoke and his son was healed in another village," a woman says to her friends.

Another voice is heard saying, "He truly is the Son of God!"

Elkan absorbs all of this as he walks with Kamali and moves his way through the crowd.

Another man is heard talking about a paralyzed man who Jesus told to walk and he did.

"Who is this man?"

"He is Jesus of Nazareth."

"The son of Joseph the carpenter?"

"The son of David!"

"Is He the Messiah?"

"The rabbis have asked Him many tough questions and He answers them all."

"He even challenges the priests of their knowledge and understanding of scripture."

"Did you hear Him when He said, 'for had you believed Moses, you would have believed me, for he wrote of me. But if you believe not his writings, how shall you believe my words?' What do you think He meant by that?"

"He truly is the Son of God!"

The conversations just continue. Elkan is quietly soaking it all in. They travel most of the day until they come to a desert place where the crowds are gathering and Jesus is healing the sick. As it is late in the day, the disciples start telling everyone to leave but Jesus tells them "No!" Then Jesus asks one of the disciples, "Philip, where will we buy bread, so that these people may eat?"

The disciple, Philip, answers Him, "Two hundred pennies worth of bread is not enough for them that every one of them may have a little."

Another disciple says to Him, "There is a lad here, who has five barley loaves, and two small fish, but what are they among so many?"

Then Jesus replies, "Make the men sit down."

There is a lot of grass in the area so everyone is able to sit comfortably. Then Jesus takes the loaves, and gives thanks. He distributes the bread to the disciples, and the disciples distribute it to the crowd. He does the same with the fish, giving everyone as much as they want. Finally everyone is full and Jesus says to His disciples, "Gather up the leftovers, so that nothing will be wasted."

The disciples gather together the leftovers, filling twelve baskets with the pieces from the five barley loaves. Then those in the crowd, seeing the miracle that Jesus did, say, "This is truly the Prophet who has come into the world."

The crowd starts growing restless and Jesus leaves by Himself to go further into the mountain. The crowd remains even though it is getting late, but Elkan and Kamali go back to their lodging place in Capernaum and arrive late at night.

The next morning when they arise, Jesus has already returned to town and is teaching again. Kamali tells Elkan that they can't stay today to listen but must head to another city in search for the key.

"Can't we stay just a little longer?" Elkan pleads.

"Not really, Elkan. We still have a lot to do before we can go back to the ship."

"Do we have to go back to the ship?"

"Yes Elkan, we do, and you know that."

Whining in protest, Elkan gives in because he knows Kamali is right.

Along their way out of town they pass by where Jesus is speaking and hear Him say, "Truly, truly, I say to you, you seek me, not because you saw the miracles, but because you ate of the loaves, and were filled. Do not labor for the meat that perishes, but for the meat that gives everlasting life, which the Son of man will give to you, for He has been preserved by God the Father."

Then the people say to Him, "What should we do, so that we might work the works of God?"

Jesus answers and says to them, "This is the work of God, that you believe in Him whom He has sent."

That is all that Elkan is able to hear as they leave the area where Jesus is speaking. They head south on a caravan route and along the way they hear people talking about Jesus and several ask them if they have heard and seen Him. The journey today is very long, and they walk the entire day and into the evening until they come upon a cave a little ways off the road and rest for the night.

The next day they continue their journey until they see in the distance a city Elkan recognizes.

"Is that Jerusalem?" he asks.

"You recognize it do you?"

"I think I recognize the temple. The one that we saw baby Jesus in. The one they were building and I liked going to visit during our stay in Jerusalem."

They hear crowds of people off to the west a short distance

away. They look to see a crowd leaving Jerusalem and gathering on a hill just outside of the city.

"Jesus must be here already. Let's go listen to Him," Elkan says excitedly, tugging on Kamali's sleeve trying to drag him behind.

So they head in the direction of the hill where the crowd is gathering. As they get closer, the crowd seems to be extremely loud this time. People are shouting and screaming and weeping. It looks like some are even throwing things.

"What's going on?" Elkan asks with a worried voice as they arrive at the base of the hill.

Clank! Clank! Clank!

Elkan hears a hammering sound and stops in his tracks with extreme fear washing over his face as he goes pale.

"This isn't ... They're not ... Jesus isn't ... being crucified is He?"

Kamali doesn't have to say a word when they see a cross rise up with a man on it. Then another. And finally, in between the first two a third one rises up.

Elkan drops to his knees and starts sobbing. "I didn't want to come here! Why? Why did you make me come here? I told you I didn't want to see this!"

Tears roll down Elkan's dusty face and puddle in the sandy dirt between his elbows as he rocks back and forth touching his head to the ground.

"He didn't do anything but tell people the truth and heal the sick and cast out demons. He made everything better. Didn't they see that? Why do they have to kill Him? Why does anyone have to kill anyone?" Elkan continues.

The noise of the crowd ebbs and flows with the rising and falling of emotions.

They hear Jesus say, "Father, forgive them for they do not know what they do." And later He says, "I thirst."

As Elkan looks up, he sees a soldier raising a spear with a sponge on the point up to Jesus' mouth and rubbing his lips with it as the liquid is squeezed from the sponge and down the front of Jesus.

They can hear the voices of one of the other men on a cross mocking Jesus. "If you are Christ, save yourself and us."

Then the man on the other cross reprimands him saying, "Do you not fear God, seeing that you are convicted the same as He is? And we are here justly, getting what we deserve, but this man has done nothing wrong!" Then he says to Jesus, "Lord, remember me when you enter your kingdom."

And Jesus replies, "Truly I say to you, today you shall be with me in paradise."

The sky darkens to where even the sun is blocked out. The earth is in darkness. Kamali places his hand on Elkan and motions him to rise to his feet. Elkan does and then buries his face into Kamali's shoulder, sobbing hard.

From the top of the hill they hear the voice of Jesus cry out, "Father, into your hands I deliver my spirit!" and Elkan slumps in Kamali's arms. He knows it is over. The end. Jesus is dead.

The earth rumbles and then quakes as rocks split and the temple behind them in the city of Jerusalem shakes. Elkan looks at Kamali for guidance on what to do and where to go. So Kamali takes him by the shoulder and they leave and find a place outside of the city to rest for the night.

For the next three days they stay in Jerusalem. They go to see where Jesus' tomb is and the temple to see any damage that might have been done from the earthquake. Many homes were also destroyed in the quake just like at Babylon. It seems to be relatively quiet in the city. There are no crowds gathering to hear Jesus speak, nor any of the disciples for that matter. The disciples are nowhere to be seen. Many people are busy cleaning up their homes and their city. The church leaders are cleaning up the temple. Life is different in Jerusalem now.

The entire time Elkan ponders what he has experienced and continually asks why? Why did Jesus have to die? Kamali doesn't tell him anything other than to think it through–that Elkan knows the answer.

The cave where Elkan and Kamali are staying happens to be near the tomb where Jesus was laid. Toward the end of the third day, which happens to be the Sabbath, or day of rest, close to dawn, there is another earthquake.

Kamali quickly grabs Elkan, and they rush to the tomb. What they witness is beyond Elkan's imagination. They see some women standing at the tomb. The stone in front of the tomb is rolled away and a figure is sitting on top of the stone. The figure reminds Elkan of the cherubim at the edge of the Garden of Eden because he looks like lightning, but his clothing is pure white like snow.

Then they hear the figure say to the women, "Do not fear! I know that you seek Jesus who was crucified. He is not here because He has risen as He said he would. Come see the place where the Lord lay, then go quickly and tell His disciples that He has risen from the dead. He goes ahead of you to Galilee. There you shall see Him as I have told you."

Then the women run back to the city. Elkan and Kamali follow them and along the way the women see Jesus who asks, "Woman, why do you cry? Whom do you seek" The women, realizing who He is, fall to the ground and worship Him at His feet.

Elkan is in shock, seeing a dead man walking and he asks Kamali "Wasn't he dead? Even if he wasn't, how could he have moved the stone–how could he even be walking or have his battered body healed?"

"Elkan … " Kamali starts.

"Duh ... He has risen from the dead. I know that! But I didn't think that He *really* rose from the dead. I just thought that people had illusions of Him or something. So it *is* real! He really *did* defeat death! How awesome!"

They hear Jesus say, "Do not be afraid, go tell my brethren to go to Galilee and they will see me there."

With that, the women continue into the city. Kamali grabs Elkan and turns the other way.

"Aren't we going to follow them?"

"No, we are going to Galilee as Jesus has instructed the disciples."

They feel a warm breeze brush them and it feels comforting. They head immediately to Galilee, traveling through the night. The next day, after taking a little rest, Elkan and Kamali see the disciples and follow them into a mountain. There they all see Jesus and worship Him, but some doubt what they see.

Then Jesus says to them, "All power is given to me in heaven and in earth. Therefore, go and teach all nations, baptizing them in the name of the Father, and of the Son, and of the Holy Spirit. Teach them to observe everything that I have commanded, and remember, I am with you always—Even until the end of the world." Then Jesus turns and walks into the mountain.

"What did He mean by that?" Elkan asks.

"He has given the disciples the power to work miracles and do what He did. He told them to teach everyone in the world, not just the Jews, and baptize them. He tells the disciples to teach those who aren't Jews about Him and to follow Him and that He will be with them in the form of the Holy Spirit always, until the end of the world."

"Wow! That would be awesome! I'd love to work miracles and heal people."

"With great power comes great responsibility. The disciples will die to themselves so that they can live for Christ. That is what He meant by the narrow gate."

All the disciples start talking to each other and Kamali nudges Elkan to head back down the mountain. "There is one place we have not been yet, and we need to get there. It is a day's journey to a city called Bethany."

"What will we see there? Will we find the key?"

"You will know in a couple of days."

They start back toward Jerusalem, but this time they bypass the city and head east. Bethany is about as far from Jerusalem as Bethlehem. When they arrive, they find a place to rest because they have had very little over the past several days. Kamali wants to make sure that Elkan rests up before whatever is going to happen in Bethany happens.

After a couple of days of rest, Elkan feels refreshed, and they go to a place called Mount Olivet. There they see the disciples with Jesus and hear them talking.

One disciple asks, "Lord, is it at this time You are restoring the kingdom to Israel?"

And Jesus replies, "It is not for you to know times or events which the Father has fixed by His own authority, but you will receive power when the Holy Spirit has come upon you. And you shall be My witnesses both in Jerusalem, and in all Judea and Samaria, and even to the remotest part of the earth." Then Elkan sees Jesus' eyes make contact with his.

After that, Jesus is lifted into the air and a cloud beneath Him carries Him into the sky and out of sight.

Two men dressed in white suddenly appear among them and say, "Men of Galilee, why do you stand looking into the sky? This Jesus, who has been taken up from you into heaven, will come in just the same way as you have watched Him go into heaven."

The disciples turn and leave, and Elkan turns to Kamali and says, "Is that it?"

"What do you mean is that it?"

"Well, me and many others thought He was dead but He rose from the grave, which I should have known would happen but was blinded by the moment of His crucifixion. Now it appears He has risen into heaven, but has He? Was that His final appearance and is He now in heaven forever?"

"Did you not hear the two men, the angels?"

Elkan sits next to a tree and looks into the sky and thinks. He thinks about everything that he saw and has learned. The reality of what has happened slowly sinks into Elkan's brain. He tries remembering what he had learned in Sunday school and processes it with everything that has happened.

Elkan gets a huge grin on his face and begins to glow with joy.

"Prophesy!" Elkan says out loud. "A lot of the old testament talks about prophesy and tells of the coming Messiah. That Messiah is Jesus. He knew He was going to be killed on the cross because He knows everything from the beginning to the end. He is the Creator, the Alpha and the Omega, the Beginning and the End. He chose to go to the cross to take the penalty of our sin—my sin—the sin that we are born into from Adam as we are all descendants of Adam." By this time Elkan is on his feet and talking loudly. "Because He took the sin himself and conquered death, we don't have to fear death. The only power Satan has over us is death, and Jesus took the key to that power from him, so we don't have to fear death at all." By now Elkan is pacing around in circles, almost lecturing. "When we die we will go to heaven, and when God judges us He will see Jesus in those who believe in Him so our sins are washed away. And there's no reason why anyone should not believe in Him because everything that the Bible says is true.

It's not stories! It's history! And not only that, it's all God's revealed word. He knows the past, present and future so why wouldn't He be able to tell us about it accurately? The Bible does just that." Then Elkan screams out, "It's true! It's all true! It's a miracle! Just as Jesus said, 'observe everything that I have commanded and remember, I am with you always—Even until the end of the world.' All we have to do is obey God and let the Holy Spirit, which is God, live in us, and He will never leave us. I can't believe it, Kamali, it all makes complete sense now. I see the truth! Jesus is truth and the Bible is truth!"

Kamali listens, grinning from ear to ear. "You have come a long way Elkan. You have grown a lot and I'm proud of you." Kamali embraces Elkan with a great big hug and pat on the back.

"Ouch!" exclaims Elkan. "What just stabbed me in the chest?"

Elkan moves away just enough to look at Kamali and he sees a piece of metal sticking through his tunic.

"What is that thing? I think that's what stabbed me in the chest." Elkan says pointing to the piece of metal.

"You have seen the truth Elkan," Kamali tells him as he pulls a leather string off from around his neck.

Dangling from the string is a shiny silver key. There are no teeth on the key though, just a shaft and back.

"You've had it all along?" Elkan accuses. "Why didn't you tell me? I wouldn't have had to go through all of this." And he pauses, "but I wouldn't change it for anything! I have learned the greatest lesson of my life."

Kamali smiles while placing the key around Elkan's neck and says, "I know." Then he places his arm around Elkan and they start back to the ship.

Night falls before they arrive back at the ship, but Elkan doesn't care. He's feeling so awake and alive he wants to continue until they get there. So they travel on through the night, with Elkan dancing and jumping and singing, and late the next day they arrive back at the dinghy and row back to the ship.

This time Elkan grabs Kamali by the arm, drags him to the captain's quarters, rushes in, and quickly drops down on his knees at the chest. He opens his ditty bag, pulls out the keys again, and opens the locks in sequence. When he gets to the sixth one, the one with the dome shape, he takes the key from around his neck and inserts it into the center of the donut hole. It doesn't go in far when the lock easily drops open. Elkan lets out a loud shout, "*Yes!*"

Then he thinks for a split second and tries to lift the far corner of the chest where the first lock is to get a peak at what's inside. Much to his disappointment, the lid won't budge. "Oh man!" he exclaims. "I thought I might be able to get a peek."

"Did you really think you'd be able to?"

"No, but I thought I'd give it a try."

Just as he has every time in the past, Kamali opens up the safe and retrieves the map. He places it on the table and unrolls it. Elkan jumps up and runs to the table to see what's new on the map.

The map is suddenly full of stuff, even from previous legs of the journey. It is loaded with thousands of different cities and images. There is so much that the map almost looks multidimensional–like there are ten different layers. There is only one area that is empty, and that's the part they haven't been to yet, the seventh sea, the Sea of Consummation.

"What does that mean?" Elkan asks pointing to the name of the seventh sea.

"It means the ultimate end - The end of all things. When God brings his kingdom to earth and makes all things new, ending the earth, as we know it."

"So that is the future?" Elkan states with a questioning tone.

"Yes, and I will say no more!"

By this point Elkan is getting tired and decides to go to bed. He is incredibly tired and his mind is on other things. He forgets to remove his keys from the locks and lock the chest back up.

Chapter 7

THE KEY

That night Elkan dreams of seeing Jesus returning on a cloud and he has a conversation with Him. Jesus tells him that He was always there with him on the journey. He was there in the forest during Creation Week, and He was there when they watched Adam and Eve sacrifice the lamb, and it was He who commanded the flood and He who came down and destroyed the tower at Babel. And He saw him admiring Him as a babe in the temple and He saw him in the crowds and behind the disciples when He taught. He saw him eat three helpings of fish and His bread. He was there when Elkan was thrust into Kamali's door and knocked unconscious.

Elkan asks Him, "So why did you choose *me* to take this quest?"

And Jesus replies, "I call everyone, Elkan, but not everyone chooses to take the journey and follow Me."

"But why not? Why wouldn't someone want to have what You can offer them?"

"Many are too blind to see the truth and their hearts are

too hard and prideful to accept my grace and mercy. My heart yearns for those lost sheep who have gone astray, but many of them have chosen death over life."

"So how can I help you find those lost sheep?"

"Tell them the truth. Tell everyone everything you know about me. And even still, show them the abundant life I offer. Never back down on My word. Never add to My word nor take away from it. Let My love shine through you."

And Jesus fades back into the sky as Elkan gently wakes up.

Elkan feels the most peaceful and at rest as he ever has. He gets up and follows his usual routine going upstairs and looking for Kamali at the bow of the ship. The air is fresh and pure. The waves are calm. Everything seems just as it was when the journey started, before everything got corrupted. Gulls are flying overhead and Kamali yells out to Elkan, "Did you sleep well?"

"Yes, I did. And I had a wonderful dream."

"It wasn't about finding the last key was it, or losing the first six?"

"What do you mean?" He asks as he reaches for his ditty bag. "Where is it?" Elkan exclaims in utter fear. "Where's my bag?" And he rushes toward the hatch to go check his room.

"Don't worry Elkan!" Kamali yells to him. "You left it in my room. And you left all of the keys in the locks–open."

"I'm so sorry! I didn't mean to. I've taken good care of them until now and then I try messing it up."

"It's okay. Everything is fine. You were tired and at least they were left in my safe keeping. You didn't 'try' to mess anything up. Don't worry about it."

"I still know better."

"Don't worry about it."

"How long until we're there?" Elkan asks changing the subject.

"How long until we're where?"

"The final stop to get the seventh and last key. The Sea of Consummation."

Kamali walks up to Elkan, places his hands on his shoulders, looks him square in the eye and says, "There is no final stop to get the seventh key, Elkan."

"What do you mean there's no stop? How do you expect me to get the key?" Elkan pauses. "Ah, I get it. The final stop isn't to get the key, it's to deliver the chest to the owner because he has the last key."

"No, Elkan. There is no final stop for any key. The Sea of Consummation is in the future and you can't travel there. Only God knows the timing for revealing the New Jerusalem, and that will be Consummation."

"So what is the New Jerusalem and what does it have to do with the Sea of Consummation?"

"Have a seat, Elkan."

Elkan goes over to his usual spot at the base of the mainmast and sits up against it.

"The New Jerusalem," Kamali begins, "is the city in which God will reside when He establishes His kingdom on the new earth. There will be no more suffering and no more pain. There will be no more death. Not a tear will fall from a single eye. He will make all things new. The city will descend out of heaven and is the bride of the lamb–the lamb being Christ. And remember, Christ will also descend out of heaven. This will be the final end."

"But if we can't go there how do I get the key?"

"You already know where the key is. You don't have it yet, but you know how to get it."

"How am I supposed to know *how* to get it when I don't even know *where* it is?"

"Because you have been told. You even said it yourself. You just have to remember."

"If you know where it is then why won't you tell me?"

"It is not for me to find. This is not my journey and you still have one last truth to realize before you find it." Kamali continues, "Think about it. Walk through what you were saying under the olive tree after Jesus rose to heaven. Think and remember. You were spitting out lots of truths. One of those truths is the answer to your question."

Elkan strains his brain trying to remember everything he said. After several moments of hitting his head against the mainmast, he starts to remember.

"Jesus died for our sins ... so that Satan no longer has power over us ... because Jesus took that power from him ... by conquering death ... and therefore ... " Elkan's voice gets a little more excitement in it. "Jesus holds the key. That's it! Jesus holds the key!"

And Elkan scrambles to his feet running as fast as he can to the hatch, flings it open, jumps down to the lower level and takes off down the corridor to Kamali's room. He reaches to fling open Kamali's door and runs smack into it. In his excitement Elkan forgot that Kamali usually keeps his door locked.

Lying flat out on the floor and holding his face, Elkan opens his eyes and looks through his fingers to see Kamali standing above him laughing.

While Elkan is picking himself up off the floor, he says, "I'm okay!" to assure Kamali he's not hurt too badly. "At least I won't have to worry about that in the New Jerusalem," he laughs.

Kamali opens the door and Elkan rushes over to the chest. He looks at the last lock and studies it. It is gold with beautiful colorful stones embedded in it. It is cube shaped and each side has three lines of multiple symbols–like hieroglyphics. This time he can read it and it contains three names on each side. One side has the names Judah, Issachar, and Zebulun. The second side has the names Reuben, Simeon, Gad. The third side has the names Ephraim, Manasseh, and Benjamin. The last side has the names Dan, Asher, and Naphtali. The top is encrusted in the same colorful stones and the bottom contains the keyhole.

Then he looks at the previous lock and studies it. It is made of stone and is dome-shaped. A second, donut-shaped stone is in the middle and is almost the size of the lock itself. The donut hole is the keyhole.

He tries pushing the key in further and that doesn't work. He tries turning the key in both directions and that doesn't work. He removes the key and tries it in the seventh lock and that doesn't work.

Standing over him, Kamali suggests thinking about the process of what he realized above deck.

Elkan thinks about how Jesus defeated death. He knows that the lock looks like the tomb, so how does the key help him show that Jesus defeated death other than by opening the tomb.

"That's it!" Elkan sticks the key into the sixth lock again and tries pushing on the donut to slide it out of the way. As he is trying this he is mumbling, "Jesus holds the key because he defeated death, and if this lock is like the tomb then the next key to Consummation is inside the tomb." When that doesn't work he tries one last idea, and that is to use the key to slide the stone out of the way.

There is a little give and then the stone slides out of the way revealing a hollow lock. Elkan looks inside and sees a key and pulls it out. It is pure gold like clear glass. Elkan inserts it into the seventh lock and looks back at Kamali who is smiling. He turns the key and the lock opens.

Elkan jumps up and starts dancing and jumping around. Then Kamali says, "Well, are you going to open it?"

Elkan removes the locks and places his hands on the front side of the lid and gives a push. It moves with ease and a bright light comes from inside. Elkan opens the lid the entire way and is consumed by the brightest light. He can't see anything around him, and especially not inside the chest. But he hears Kamali's voice say, "Behold, the Shekinah Glory of God!" Elkan reaches into the chest and grabs hold of something. When he gets his hands around it and starts to pull it out, he hears another voice calling his name.

"Elkan! Elkan, are you alright? What's taking you so long? I was worried about you down here with the electricity having gone out."

The voice is that of Mrs. Brown and Elkan looks behind him to see her coming down the steps of the church basement. He looks back at his hands, and he is holding a large and very old book.

"Mrs. Brown! You won't believe it, but I just took the most amazing journey of my life!"

And Mrs. Brown looks at the book in his hand and replies with a big grin, "Yep! The Bible is full of great adventures. It's not just a book of stories you know?"

"I know! Everything in it is true! And you can believe every word of it!"

"Yes you can, Elkan. It's a journey you just have to be willing to take."

Meet the Authors:

John has a bachelor's degree in Journalism with a minor in Marketing. He is the Marketing Coordinator for a non-profit organization in Northern Kentucky. Kathy has been a stay at home mom for the past ten years. They live with their two sons, Evan and James, near Cincinnati.

John and Kathy consider their children of utmost importance and desire for them to think for themselves instead of blindly following everything that the world tells them. Their greatest joy is knowing that their children walk in the truth.